Dangerous Space

Also by Kelley Eskridge

Solitaire

Dangerous Space

Short fiction by
Kelley Eskridge

Seattle

Aqueduct Press, PO Box 95787
Seattle, WA 98145-2787
www.aqueductpress.com

Library of Congress Control Number: 2007923221
ISBN: 978-1-933500-13-3
ISBN: 1-933500-13-1
First Edition, First Printing, June 2007
15 14 13 12 11 10 09 08 07   1 2 3 4 5

PUBLICATION ACKNOWLEDGMENTS
"Strings" first appeared in *The Magazine of Fantasy and Science Fiction*, February 1994. Copyright © 1994 by Kelley Eskridge. "And Salome Danced" first appeared in *Little Deaths* (Ellen Datlow, editor). UK: Orion. Copyright © 1994 by Kelley Eskridge. "City Life," originally published as "The Hum of Human Cities," first appeared in *Pulphouse: A Hardback Magazine*, Vol. 9, 1990. Copyright © 1990 by Kelley Eskridge. "Eye of the Storm" first appeared in *Sirens and Other Daemon Lovers* (Ellen Datlow, editor) USA: HarperPrism, 1998. Copyright © 1998 by Kelley Eskridge. "Somewhere Down the Diamondback Road" first appeared in *Pulphouse: A Fiction Magazine*, Issue 15, 1993. Copyright © 1993 by Kelley Eskridge. "Alien Jane" first appeared in *Century Magazine*, Vol. 1, 1995. Copyright © 1995 by Kelley Eskridge.

Cover painting *La Despedida*
Remedios Varo   Spain 1908 – Mexico 1963
Photograph courtesy Walter Gruen
Cover and Book Design by Kathryn Wilham

Printed in the USA by Thomson-Shore, Inc, Dexter, MI
This book was set in a digital version of Monotype Walbaum, available through AGFA Monotype. The original typeface was designed by Justus Erich Walbaum.

for Nicola, my heart

Contents

Acknowledgments

Thanks very much to the editors who liked these
stories enough to publish them, especially Ellen
Datlow, Rob Killheffer, and Kris Rusch. And now,
of course, the fantastic people of Aqueduct—
Timmi Duchamp, Tom Duchamp, Kath Wilham,
and Melanie Madden.

Thanks to my Clarion instructors, whose lessons I
am still learning all these years later, especially Tim
Powers and Chip Delany.

And thank you to Nicola, who makes me better than
I might otherwise be.

Introduction
by Geoff Ryman

There are no politics anymore.

There's mudslinging, covert operations, aerial bombardment, helpless or hopeless diplomacy, vote rigging, private detectives digging dirt on candidates for other candidates not worthy of respect, US Presidents who can't be bothered to pronounce correctly the name of an allied head of state, dictators hanged for real crimes before they can reveal crimes we sponsored, communists turned gangsters, and news so slanted that anchormen roll their eyes when the opposition talks.

What's lacking are coherent, systematized ideologies that form a basis for action. Unless you count the culture-war attempt to make the USA a theocracy.

Yet all the great givens—morality, religion, and liberation politics—are where we came from. We've moved beyond these things (or did they move away from us?). But they are still part of us.

Kelley Eskridge's stories are in some fundamental way to do with politics, religion, and morality, but homeopathically. These things like remedies leave the shape of their molecules behind in the water, their outline.

4

Politics are a tincture in her stories, most notable for their absence. "Strings" is a story about new music forcing its way out of an imagined cultural fascism. In this world, children only know classical music. Musical originality is a crime, a perversion, swiftly punished by thuggish authority. Could this story exist without a political awareness? No. But it almost seems to be about helplessness in the face of politics. Art here is a triumph of the spirit, a final venting of the self in times even more insalubrious than our own. "Strings" is also, like all of Eskridge's work, beautifully and simply written, with individual sentences of resounding beauty. She communicates so simply the clammy breath of fascism. And look how lightly she shows us how this world works—a textbook example of how to show a setting.

Art is also the background of "And Salome Danced." The process of putting on a play, the ebb and flow of teamwork and tension, is convincingly caught. What's striking about this story is that it is post-queer. Twenty years ago a story like this would have used gender-bending to destabilize conventional perception. Now gender-bending is itself conventional, and this story uses it entirely neutrally for no political ends at all. Joe/Jo is some kind of vampire, but what s/he sucks is talent not blood. The shape-shifting, gender-bending can be good or it can be evil. But how would we read the story without the legacy of gay and then queer politics?

These tales are post-vanilla. Nobody is vanilla these days, at least not in their heads. Extreme sex and extreme violence are the norm in entertainment. In "Somewhere Down the Diamondback Road," drugs, lascivious and yet state-sponsored murder, the freedom of the road, and a love of language make a potent and poisonous cocktail. This for me is the most powerfully written of the stories. Style goes so far that it becomes substance.

We live in an age when one of the most influential works of art is *Fight Club*. The enjoyment of violence is in the air we breathe. In "The Eye of the Storm," a mercenary discovers that s/he is only able to have a sexual response when fighting, as if hammering and rending is the only way to penetrate a person. This story makes you ponder why young men yearn to touch each other with their fists and why young women so routinely dream of being warriors. It is taken as read that people enjoy sex with both genders, that polyandry works, and that women fight as well as men. These are not issues, just background.

Religion haunts these stories too. Jo/e could play either John the Baptist or Salome to shattering effect. S/he's less interested in Mary Magdalene. There is a Magdalena in "City Life" as well, and like Jesus, she can heal the sick. Only post-religion, even this is not an unmitigated good. Goodness disrupts the system. As she heals, so the City starts to fall apart. Windows drop from skyscrapers, sewers open up under sidewalks. The City itself swirls into the shape of a bag lady to bring disrupting goodness to a halt.

Because Eskridge is moving on from the new conventions, her images are unfamiliar. The bag lady is not an object of sympathy or sentiment or social outrage. Magdalena finds sainthood unbearable. The City is decayed but not the unmitigated hell hole that it would have been in a story written thirty years ago. Eskridge is freshly neutral about a range of topics that not so long ago were controversial and cutting edge.

In "Alien Jane," all of this is twisted round on its head. We are suddenly in the past, the time of *Remington Steele* where the feminist tales of independent women shut away in asylums for not wearing high heels are given a new lease on life through 21st century eyes. Love starts out as a desire by one woman to really hurt another. Yet freedom suddenly simply walks out the front door to find itself.

This is a very canny moment on which to end the collection. It's as if we had stumbled accidentally onto hope and wholesome, effective action.

Fictionality is constantly acknowledged, but never directly referred to. The sheer genre-ality of these tales, their abiding inside genre, means they lead us out of genre. Eskridge samples matters and then renders them irrelevant.

The *Mad Max*-ish Diamondback Road, the nostalgia for feminist fiction in "Alien Jane," the sword and sorcery background of "The Eye of the Storm," and the horror elements in "And Salome Danced" and "City Life"— genre matters is the water in which Eskridge's remedies infuse. Drink deep and discover that though this brew's flavor is anything other than vanilla, you believe in goodness after all.

What then?

Then there is "Dangerous Space."

There is a moment in the careers of artists, when they cease to be innovative, quirky, promising, or off the wall, and become traditional, or perhaps I should say, classic. It's the moment when kick-out-the-jams formalism and a fervor for style subsides to be replaced by simple clarity. The moment when U2 got over *Boy* and started to record "Pride (In the Name of Love)." When you find your goodness and a measure of peace, you stop being pouty and punky. "Dangerous Space" is a story, curiously, about that moment in music when you go from the Cavern Club to Ed Sullivan. It makes you think, this woman could be making movies. She could SO tell an actor what lies beneath the face they must not move. She could be SO making music, either on a violin or guitar, but she writes instead, and this anthology is a record of how she kept crossing borders only to find her way home.

It's a love story, and love stories have happy endings.

Strings

She took the stage, head shaking. Her jaw and the tiny muscles in her neck rippled in sharp adrenaline tremors. She moved her head slowly back and forth while she walked the twenty yards from stage right to the spotlight; it was always the same, this swooping scan, taking in the waiting orchestra, the racks of lights overhead, the audience rumbling and rustling. She moved her head not so much to hide the shaking as to vent it: to hold it until center stage and the white-light circle where she could raise the violin, draw it snug against the pad on her neck; and at the moment of connection she looked at the Conductor and smiled, and by the time he gathered the orchestra into the waiting breath of the upraised baton, she had become the music once again.

After the final bows, she stood behind the narrow curtain at the side of the stage and watched the audience eddy up the aisles to the lobby and the street and home. She could tell by their gentle noise that the current of the music carried them for these moments as it had carried her for most of her life.

Nausea and exhaustion thrust into her like the roll of sticks on the kettledrum. And something else, although she did not want to acknowledge it: the thinnest whine of a string, phantom music high and wild in a distant, deep place within her head.

"Excuse me, Strad?"

She jerked, and turned. The orchestra's First Clarinet stood behind her, a little too close.

"I'm sorry." He reached out and almost touched her. "I didn't mean to startle you."

"No. No, it's okay." She felt the tension in her smile. "Was there something you wanted?" Her right hand rubbed the muscles of her left in an old and practiced motion.

"Oh. Yes. The party has started; we were all wondering... You are coming to the party, aren't you?"

She smiled again, squared her shoulders. She did not know if she could face it: the percussion of too many people, too much food, the interminable awkward toasts they would make to the Stradivarius and the Conservatory. She had seen a Monitor in the house tonight, and she knew he would be at the party too, with a voice-activated computer in his hands; they would be soft, not musician's hands. She wondered briefly how big her file was by now. She wanted desperately to go back to the hotel and sleep.

"Of course," she said. "Please go back and tell them I'll be there just as soon as I've changed." Then she found her dressing room and began, unsteadily, to strip the evening from herself.

❧

She was tense and tired the next morning as she
packed her music and violin and clothes. Her next guest
solo was with an orchestra in a city she had not visited for
several years. A Conservatory limo picked her up at the
airport along with the current Guarnerius, who handed
his cello into the back seat as if it were an aging grande
dame rather than hardwood and almost half his weight.
He was assigned to the same orchestra, but only for two
weeks. She was glad she would have a week alone with
the musicians after he left. She did not like him.

He chattered at her all the way to the hotel, mis-
taking her silence for attention. She tried to listen, to
allow him to bore her or anger her, to distract her. But
she could not hook her attention onto him: it slid away
like the rain down the windshield of the car, dropped
into the steady beat of the tires on the wet road, *thud-
DUH thud-DUH*, the rhythm so familiar and comfort-
ing that she relaxed into it unguardedly and was caught
and jerked into the welter of other sound that was also
the car and the road and the journey: *thwump thwump*
of the wipers, the alto ringing of the engine, the col-
oratura squeak of the seat springs as Guarnerius leaned
forward to make an earnest point, the counterpoint of
the wheels of the cars around them, *thudduh thudduh
THUMP thump-thump THUD-duh*; and no matter how
hard she tried, she could not make it something she recognized; she had no music for it. No Bach, no Paganini,
no Mozart or Lalo or Vivaldi would fit around the throb-
bing in her bones, and she was suddenly sure that if her
heart were not pounding so loud, she would hear that

distant wailing music in her head, it would wind around her like a woman dancing, sinuous, sweating, swaying, wrapping her up—

She jerked. The edge of Guarnerius's briefcase pressed against her arm. She remembered G did not like to touch other people or be touched by them. She wondered if he chose to play the cello so he would never have to sit next to another passenger on an airplane. She wondered if he ever heard phantom music.

"...*waiting*, Strad." The cold rim of the briefcase pushed at her arm.

She blinked, looked up at him.

"We're here, for God's sake. The whole orchestra is probably on pins and needles, poor idiots, waiting in there for the Strad and Guarnerius to arrive, and here you sit gaping off into the middle distance. Or were you planning to ask them to rehearse in the car?"

She could feel herself flush. "No," she said shortly, definitely, as if it would answer everything, and stepped out.

She never made friends easily. There were a thousand reasons: she was too shy; she was the Strad, and other people were shy of her; she was busy. Sometimes she thought she was too lonely to make friends, as if the solitude and separateness were so much a part of her that she did not know how to replace them with anything else. So it was simply another sign of how upside down things were that she found a heart-friend on the second day of rehearsal with the new orchestra. They might have been friends the first day, if he had been there.

"I'm very sorry, Stradivarius," the Stage Manager said. She was a thick-set woman with a clipboard and a pinch-eyed look. She was also, Strad thought, worried and not hiding it as well as she wished.

"I'm very sorry," the SM began again. "I'm afraid we can't rehearse the Viotti this afternoon as planned."

Strad rubbed her left hand with her right. She wished for one improbable moment that the SM would give her an excuse to fly into a rage so that she could howl out all her fear and tension safely disguised as artist's pique. But she could not: all other considerations aside, it reminded her too much of something G might do.

She sighed. "What seems to be the problem? My schedule requests were quite clear."

"Yes, Stradivarius. But our Piano isn't here."

"Then get someone over to the nearest bar or video-house or wherever she or he...he?...wherever he is and bring him along."

"It's not like that. He..." The SM swallowed. "He's at a Conservatory disciplinary hearing. We're not sure if he's coming back or not...but we don't want to replace him until we're sure, because it's not fair." She stopped, gripped the clipboard tighter against her breasts. "I beg your pardon," she said formally. "I did not intend to question the decisions of the Conservatory. The entire orchestra apologizes for the inconvenience caused by one of our members."

"Oh, put a sock in it," Strad said, surprising them both. "What's he done?"

"He's been accused of improvising."

He was back the next day. Strad knew it the moment she walked into the hall for the morning rehearsal. The room seemed brighter, as if there were more light and air in it than the day before.

She saw him in the midst of a crowd of players, like a young sapling in the sun. From habit, she noticed his hands first. They were thin and strong-looking, with long, square-tipped fingers; expressive hands. *Good*, she thought, and looked next at his face.

He's so young. His eyes and mouth moved with the same emotion as his hands, but none of the control. Someone touched his shoulder, and as he turned, laughing, he saw Strad watching him. His eyes widened, the laugh turned into a beautiful smile; then, quite suddenly, he looked away. It jolted her, as if a string had broken in mid-note.

She felt movement behind her. Guarnerius appeared at her left shoulder, with the Conductor in tow.

"Is that him?"

"Yes, Guarnerius."

"What did the disciplinary committee decide to do about him?"

"He's on probation. He's been warned." The Conductor shrugged. "I couldn't prove anything, you see; it was just a matter of a few notes. They really couldn't do anything except cite him for faulty technique." The Conductor sounded unconcerned; Strad thought committee hearings were probably all in a day's work for her. No wonder the orchestra was tense. No wonder their Piano was playing forbidden notes. She could imagine herself in his place, young and impatient, aching to prove she was better than the music she was given to play, knowing that one note added here or there would support the piece and give it more resonance, wanting to hear how it might sound... And then she did hear.

It started slow and soft, the music in her head. It swirled through her skull like a thread of heavy cream in hot coffee. It seeped down her spine. *I mustn't move*, Strad thought. *If I can just not move, it won't know I'm here, and it will go back wherever it came from.* The almost-audible music bubbled in her bones. *Go find someone else to play with!* she thought wildly. Then she looked again at the Piano, and knew it had.

"How soon can you find someone else?" Guarnerius's voice grated against the music. For a confused moment, she wondered if he were talking about her, and a huge, voiceless *no* swelled inside her.

"I have no grounds to replace him," the Conductor said.

G shrugged. "Contract privilege. If Strad and I find him unacceptable, you're obligated to provide a substitute."

"There isn't going to be anyone as good..."

"There isn't going to be any substitute," Strad interrupted.

"What are you talking about?" Guarnerius looked sharply into her eyes, but she knew the Conductor was looking at her shaking hands.

"He was warned, G, not expelled."

"He was improvising."

"The Conservatory apparently doesn't have reason to think so. Besides, what's the point of upsetting everyone again? We've already missed a day's rehearsal, and your Strauss is difficult enough without having the orchestra tense and angry and playing badly."

Guarnerius frowned. Strad turned back to the Conductor, who was managing to look attentive and unobtrusive all at once. Strad could feel her hands still trembling slightly. She folded them carefully in front of her, knowing the Conductor saw.

"Perhaps you'll be kind enough to gather the players?"

"Perhaps you'd like a moment to yourself before rehearsal?" The other woman's voice was carefully neutral. Strad wanted to break something over her lowered head.

"No, I would not," she said, very precisely. "What I would like is a few moments with my music and a full orchestra, if that can be arranged sometime before opening night."

The Conductor flushed. "My apologies, Stradivarius."

"Well, let's get on with it," G said crossly.

She did not get to speak with the Piano until the next day. She sat on the loading dock at the back of the hall during the midday break, enjoying the sun and the solitude. She was far enough from the street that no mechanical noises reached her: she heard only the creak of the metal loading door in the breeze, the muffled, brassy warble of trumpet scales, the hissing wind in the tall grass of the empty lot behind the building. The sun was warm and red on her closed eyelids. A cricket began to fiddle close by.

"I thought you might like some tea."

The cricket stopped in mid-phrase. She felt suddenly angry at the endless stream of infuriating and intrusive courtesies that were offered to the Strad. Nevertheless, she smiled in the general direction of the voice. "You're very kind," she said. She kept her eyes closed and hoped whoever it was would put down the tea and go away.

"Well, no, I'm not. I just didn't know how else to get to talk to you."

"I'm available to any musician. It's part of being the Strad, everyone knows that. Please don't feel shy."

"I'm not shy. I just thought you might not want to be seen talking to me, considering everything."

Strad opened her eyes and sat up straight. "Oh. It's you. I didn't realize…" He stepped back. "No, please don't go," she said quickly and put one hand out. "Please. I'd like to talk to you." He came back slowly, tall, dark, close-cropped hair, those beautiful hands. He held two mugs that steamed almost imperceptibly.

"Sit down."

He handed her a cup and sat next to her on the edge of the loading dock, curling into a half-lotus, tea cradled in his lap. She took a sip and tasted hot cinnamon, orange, bright spices.

"Can I talk to you?" he said.

"Of course. I just told you…"

"No," he said quietly. "Can I talk to you?"

The rich yellow taste of the tea seeped through her. She felt transparent and warm, caught between the sun and the tea and the young man who wore his music like skin.

"Yes. You can talk to me."

He let out a long breath. Everything was still for a moment. The cricket began to play again.

"It was awful at the disciplinary committee," he said, as abruptly and comfortably as if they had known each other for years. "They would have dismissed me if they could. There was an old man with long grey hair who made me take the phrase note by note to prove that I knew how to play it. He wanted me to repeat what I had done during the rehearsal that made the Conductor charge me."

"Boethius." Strad nodded. The Piano looked at her. "He's the Master Librarian," she explained. His eyes widened and then closed for a moment.

"I suppose he does all the notation of the scores as well."

"Mmm," Strad agreed. "He doesn't like having his toes stepped on."

"Well, at least now I know why he...he really scared me. I'll never be able to play that piece again without freezing up at that movement." He grinned at her. "Don't say it: I know I'm lucky to play the piece again at all." His smile faded. He took a gulp of tea, swallowed, studied the inside of the cup. Strad stayed still, watching him.

He looked up after a while, up and beyond her into the empty field.

"I never improvised half as much in the music as I did in that room." He was silent for a moment, remembering. His fingers twitched. "You know I did it, don't you." It was not a question.

She nodded.

"Thought so. Some of my friends in there——" he looked at the hall, "——don't believe I could have done it. They wouldn't understand. They just...they play what

they're told, and they seem happy, but that's not music. It's *not*," he said again, defiantly. His cheeks were
red, and his voice shook. "So how can they be happy?"
He swallowed, took a deep breath. "Maybe they aren't.
Maybe they're just making do the best they can. I can
almost understand that now, you know, after the hearing… I wish that cricket would just shut up." He picked
up a piece of gravel from the edge of the dock and threw
it out into the field. The cricket fiddling stopped.

"What's it like, being an Instrument?"

"It's good." She saw, in a blur, all her Competitions,
all her challengers. "It's hard. It can be amazing. The
Conservatory orchestra is wonderful." She set down her
cup. "You're thinking of the Competition? Of challeng-
ing the Steinway?"

He bit his lip. "I've thought about it. Maybe we
all do…" He sighed. "I know if I ever want to be the
Steinway I'll have to…I'll stop improvising. But Strad, I
don't know how to stop the music in my head."

She felt herself go very still. She had made no sound,
but he looked up and out of himself and saw her. "Oh,"
he said gently, hopefully, sadly. "You, too?"

She found the muscles that moved her mouth. "I
don't know what—" *you're talking about*, she meant to
say, and have it finished. But she could not. She had a
sudden, clear image of how he must have looked in the
disciplinary hearing: a new suit, an old shirt, his breath
sour with anxiety, and his mouth suddenly not very
good with words. He would have appreciated the piano
they had him use, she knew; it was undoubtedly the fin-
est instrument he had ever played. She thought of him
carefully wiping the fear-sweat from his hands before

he touched it, of him playing it and denying the music he heard lurking within its strings. It broke her heart.

"I don't know what to do," she said, and behind her the cricket began to play again.

That night she dreamed of her first Competition. She stood with the other challengers backstage while a crowd of people with no faces settled into the arena seats. She played in her dream as she had in the real moment, with the passion that the music demanded and the precision that the Judges required of a Strad; as if the piece were a new, wondrous discovery, and at the same time as if she had played it a hundred thousand times before. She forgot the audience was there until they began to clap and then shout, and she could not see them clearly because she was weeping.

Then the audience disappeared, and the building vanished into a landscape of sand under a sand-colored sky. Directly ahead of her, a door stood slightly ajar in its frame. She heard her violin crying. She stumbled forward into dark. The violin screamed on and on as she searched for it. She found it, eventually, high on a shelf over the door. It went silent when she touched it. She pulled it down and hugged it to her, and fell on her knees out onto the sand.

She looked at the violin anxiously, turning it over, running her fingers across the bridge and the strings. She could not see any damage.

Suddenly a voice spoke from the darkness inside the open door. "It only looks the same," it hissed, and the door slammed shut inches from her face at the same time that the violin stood itself on end and burst into song. And then she awoke, clutching a pillow to her side and sweating in the cool air of her hotel suite.

She lay still for a few moments, then got up and went into the bathroom, filled the tub full of water so hot that she had to lower herself into it an inch at a time.

She closed her eyes as the water cooled around her neck and knees; she remembered the music that had burst from her violin at the end of her dream. She recognized it: the distant, maddening music that she had heard earlier; the haunting melody that stirred her hands to shape it; the illegal music that she could never play.

When she tried to stand up, her hand slipped on the porcelain rim, and her elbow cracked against it. The pain drove the music from her head, and she was grateful.

~≫

"Let's have a picnic," the Piano said a few days later, at the end of an afternoon's rehearsal, the rich, rolling energy of good music still in the air. There was a moment of quiet, as if everyone were trying to work out what picnics had to do with concert performances. Then the SM set down her pile of scores with a solid paperish thunk.

"That's a great idea," she said. Behind her, Guarnerius rolled his eyes and went back to packing up his cello.

The SM produced a clipboard and a pen. "Who wants to bring what?" She was surrounded by a crowd of jabbering voices and waving hands. It took a few minutes for the group to thin out enough to let Strad get close.

The SM looked up at her, obviously surprised. "Was there something you wanted, Strad?"

"I'd like to bring something, but you'll have to tell me what we need."

"Oh no, we'll take care of it, Strad. There's no need to trouble yourself."

"I'd like to." But the SM had already turned away. *Damn it*, Strad thought. She gathered up her violin and left the hall, walking alone through the double doors into the sun and smell of the street.

The limo waited alongside the curb. The driver got out and moved around the car to take her things. She gave him her violin and music, but shook her head when he opened the rear door for her.

"I'll walk. Guarnerius is still packing up, I don't know how long he'll be. Wait for me outside the hotel, and I'll pick up my things. Don't give them to anyone but me."

"Yes, Stradivarius," the driver answered. He looked at the ground while she talked, so she could not tell if he minded being told what to do. *Damn*, she thought again.

She walked fast the first few blocks. Then she realized that no one recognized her, that no one was paying her any more than casual attention, and gradually she felt safe enough to slow down. She was sweating lightly, and she stopped under a canvas awning in front of a shop to catch her breath. She pressed herself against the cool concrete of the building, out of the way of people moving along the sidewalk, and watched the world go by.

A man stood at a bus stop, absorbed in *Wuthering Heights*, humming Brahms. A couple passed her with a transistor radio, Vivaldi trickling fuzzily from the speaker. A pack of little boys on bicycles pedaled down the street, bellowing the *1812 Overture*, booming out the cannon with gleeful satisfaction. *My audience*, Strad realized with wonder. She thought of all the musicians, all the hours and the work for a few minutes of song that lived and died from one note to the next. *But they hear. They hear.*

She stepped out from the shadow and wandered up the sidewalk. It was as if the whole world had opened up since she had talked to the Piano, since she had told someone how it was with her. She saw things she had not seen in a long time: dirt, children's toys, hot food ready to eat out of paper containers, and narrow alleyways and the open back doors of restaurants where people in grubby aprons stood fanning themselves and laughing. And everywhere the music, the works of the masters, clear and rich and beautiful, the only music; the sounds and feelings that had shaped and contained her life since she was young, as young as the child who stumbled on the pavement in front of her. Strad stopped and offered her hand, but the little girl picked herself up with a snort and ran on down the street.

Strad smiled. As she craned her neck to watch the child run, she saw a smear of bright color beside her. She turned and found herself in front of a window full of lines and whorls and grinning fantastical faces that resolved into dozens of kites, all shapes and sizes and shades of color. "Oh," she breathed, catching her hands up to her ribs.

"Everybody does that," someone said, and chuckled. She saw a woman standing in the open door of the shop. Bits of dried glue and gold glitter and colored paper were stuck to her arms and clothes.

"They're beautiful," Strad said.

"Come in and have a closer look."

She left the shop with a kite bundled under her arm, light but awkward. She walked slowly; the hotel was only a few minutes away, and she wished she had farther to go so that she could enjoy herself longer.

She passed a woman who smiled and then wrinkled her eyebrows and gave Strad an odd look. It was only then she realized that, like so many others, she was humming as she walked. But the music that buzzed in her mouth was the alien music that she had thought was safely locked in her head. She knew the other woman had heard it; then she began to wonder who else might have heard, and she spun in a circle on the sidewalk, trying to look in all directions at once for someone with a hand-held recorder or a wallet with a Monitor's badge. She was sweating again. Suddenly the hotel seemed much too far away. She wished for sunglasses or a hat or the cool of the Conservatory limousine. The music lapped against the back of her tongue all the way back to her room.

The kite was an enormous success. Most of the players wanted a turn, although G and the Conductor made a point of turning up their noses when offered. The kite had a large group that leaped and shouted under it as it bobbed along in the clear sky over the park.

The Piano had brought his wife. "You're someone famous, aren't you?" she said to Strad when they were introduced. The Piano poked her sharply in the ribs. "Stop it, hon," she said calmly, and went on shaking Strad's hand. "Not everybody knows music, as I keep trying to point out to the whiz kid here. Everyone says you're very good. Did you really tell the SM to put a sock in it?" She was a tall, loose-boned woman with deep-set brown eyes. Strad liked her.

They sat on the grass and talked while the Piano joined the group running with the kite. His wife smiled as she watched him. "He was so excited about meeting you. He needs friends who understand his work. I guess you do, too."

"Yes," Strad agreed. "What do you do?" she asked, suddenly very curious.

"I teach literature to fifth graders. They all wanted to come with me today. I told them it was my turn for a field trip."

Words and music, Strad thought. *What a household they must have together.*

"What are you thinking?"

"I was just envying you," Strad said.

Later, after the others had worn themselves out, the three of them took the kite to the edge of the park green for one last flight.

"I know what it reminds me of," the Piano's wife said. "With those deep colors and the tail swirling. It looks like something the gypsies would have had, that I read to my kids about. They loved to sing and dance. I'll bet it was just like that, all dips and swirls and jumping around. They played violins, too, did you know that?" she added, with a grin for Strad. "I wonder what it sounded like."

I think I know, Strad thought.

"Careful, hon," the Piano said warningly. He jerked his chin towards the other side of the park. A man stood on a slight hill overlooking the common, staring down at the players. He carried a hand-held recorder.

"They don't leave you alone at all, do they?" his wife muttered. "At least I only have to worry about them on the job. Although I hear it's worse if you're a history teacher..." She sighed and began to reel in the kite.

They walked back to the group together, but they found separate places to sit. Strad put the kite away.

≈

"Well, I for one will be extremely glad when this particular tour is over," Guarnerius announced, and put his drink down on Strad's table. Strad wished he would just go away. It was the last night of his engagement with the orchestra, and she was heartily sick of him.

"Where do you go from here?"

"Back to the Conservatory. Time to get ready for the Competition. Well, you know that, of course." He patted at the wrinkles in his jacket. Alcohol fumes drifted from his mouth. "You should be rehearsing. What's your schedule like?"

"Well, there's next week here, and I've got one more city."

"I don't envy you another week with this miserable orchestra."

"Mmm," she said noncommittally. G's engagement had not gone well, and two clanging wrong notes in his solo that night had not improved his temper.

"Really, Strad. That Conductor is as wooden as her baton, the entire brass section needs a good kick in the rear, and that Piano... Well, small wonder they had trouble with him, considering the state of the rest of the group." He nodded, took another swallow of his drink, and set the glass down so that it clacked against the wooden table as if helping to make his point.

"I thought the Piano played very well."

"Well of course he did, Strad, don't be an idiot. He's already screwed up once, and now he's being monitored. Of course he's going to play well."

Monitored. She picked up her glass and leaned back in her chair, let her gaze wander around the room. And there he was, the same Monitor that she had seen at her last orchestra. Had he been the one at the park? Was it normal for the same Monitor to turn up again and again? She had never noticed before. She realized how much she, like the Piano, had always taken the Monitors for granted. She felt a cramp like someone's fist in her stomach. The sickness brought with it the faint, sweet music inside her skull. The Monitor's head came up like a hunting dog's, as if somehow he had heard it too. She watched him scan the room, making whispered notes into his recorder, and she saw as if through his eyes: *how scared they all look, how stiff and anxious; see a hand moving too sharply there, a voice raised slightly too high, the smell of hunger for something illegal...* Strad dropped her gaze back down into her own glass.

There was something cold and wet against her arm. "—your *problem* lately, Strad?" Guarnerius nudged her again with his glass.

"What?"

"That's exactly what I mean," he said with a smile that was not altogether nice. "You're very preoccupied lately, aren't you, dear?"

She could only stare at him in shock.

"Oh yes, I've noticed. It hasn't shown up in your music yet, but it will. Bound to. One of these fine days you'll be up on stage and your hands will slip on the strings, and then we'll see what it's like when the Strad loses that precious control, that fucking *precision* that everyone's always going on about, oh yes…" The words trailed off. Strad realized for the first time how drunk he was. She remembered that he had made bad mistakes that night, and the Monitor had been there.

Guarnerius stared into his glass as if he wanted to climb in and hide among the ice cubes. Strad stood up and grabbed her violin, music case, coat, and bag into a loose, awkward bundle. "I'm sorry, Strad," she heard him mumble, but she was already moving. She smiled and excused her way across the crowded room without seeing or hearing anything properly until she came to a wall and could go no further. There was an empty chair by the wall. She dropped her things on the floor next to it and sat down.

The chair made her invisible somehow; at least, no one approached her. The party happened in front of her, like a video. She rubbed her hands, left with right, right with left, watching the groups mingle and break apart and spiral into new forms: the currents matched the music that swelled in gentle waves in her head. And it was too much, she could not fight it any longer: somewhere inside her a door edged open, and the music trickled through.

She did not know how long she sat before she realized that someone was standing in front of her. She looked up. It was the Piano. She could not speak. He took her arm and pulled her to her feet, tugged her out a side door of the restaurant onto an open patio. He sat her hard into a wrought iron chair at one of the tables. The metal bit cold and sticky through her light dress. She opened her mouth and took in great heaving bites of air, one after the other, until she felt the door inside her push tightly closed, the music safely behind it.

The Piano sat next to her. She held his hand so hard that the ends of his fingers turned bright red.

"Oh, thank you," she whispered. "How did you know to bring me out here?"

He reached over and brushed a finger against her cheek. It came away wet. "You were crying," he said. "You were sitting in that chair, staring at nothing and crying like the loneliest person on earth, and you weren't making a sound. So I brought you outside."

She put her hands up to her face. Her skin felt puffy and hot.

"What is it?" he asked.

"It's so beautiful," she said.

And then: "I'm scared."

The morning she went to her next city, she met some of the players in the hotel to have breakfast and say goodbye. The Piano was there. She kept him in the lobby after the others left.

"I hate to say goodbye," he said.

"I have something for you," she said. She gave him the kite.

"I'll fly it for you."

She looked at him closely. "You be careful," she said.

"Don't worry."

"I mean it."

"So do I. I'll keep the kite, and every time it flies I'll be thinking of you and the music we both have in us. The trick is to keep it alive somehow. There has to be a way, Strad. There has to be a way to have it and play it and be what we are."

He stood looking at her, and she thought he would say more. But in the end he only nodded and kissed her gently on the cheek.

She went to her next city, to the rehearsals and dinners and performances and parties, and then back to the Conservatory, to the soundproofed suite of rooms and the tiny private garden that were hers for as long as she was the Stradivarius. She rested, ate, played with the other musicians, all the Instruments gathered together to face their yearly challengers. She rehearsed her Competition piece. One day, Guarnerius asked her stiltedly how her last engagement had gone.

"It went fine," she told him. "No problems."

He muttered, "Oh, how nice," and stepped around her, moved stiffly down the hallway toward one of the Conservatory practice rooms. She wondered how he would have reacted if she had told him that she had played as well as ever, and that it had all been empty: hollow, meaningless sound.

It was a relief to put her violin away when she got back to her rooms. There were letters on the desk. There were instructions and announcements from the Conservatory. There was a note from the Conductor of an orchestra she had guested with once before. There was a package from the Piano.

The note was unsigned: he would know that her mail might be monitored. She did not realize it was from him until she opened the package and saw the kite. She put it slowly on the desk and set the note beside it on the polished wood. She read it again without touching it. A little of the silence inside her gave way to the remembered sound of his voice.

> I am sending you this as an admirer of your work and your talent. The beauty of this kite reminds me of the music you carry within you, that you as the Strad keep in trust for us all. I have been told recently, by those who love me best and who watch me closely, that I can no longer risk flying it myself, as it is too strenuous and dangerous to my health. I will miss it. I would not suggest you fly it, but it is beautiful to look at.

She folded the note into a small rectangle and tucked it inside her shirt, against her skin. She thought about the Piano running in the park, whooping and pointing at the kite. Then she went out of her rooms into the garden and pushed a chair into the sun, sat and closed her eyes against the light, and let the silence fill her up.

She stayed in her rooms for the next four weeks, rehearsing for the Competition. Her practice was painstaking. She wrung the piece dry. Every note, every phrase, every rest was considered and balanced. Every nuance of tone and meaning was polished until the notes seemed to shine as they shot from the strings.

She felt hollow and open, as wide and empty as a summer sky. She slept without dreaming. She spoke only when necessary. She touched everything gently, as if she had never known texture before.

The night of the Competition, she waited calmly in the wings. The challengers stared at her, or tried not to. She smelled their sweat. One of them, a young woman with lion-gold hair, was very good. Strad smiled encouragingly at her when she came offstage, and the young woman smiled back with all the joy of accomplishment, and then blushed desperately.

The Assistant Stage Manager came to her. "Five minutes, please, Stradivarius," he said, and gave her a little bow and smile that meant *good luck*. She rose and walked to the place that she would enter from. Through the gap in the curtains, she could see the Judges frowning over their evaluations of the challengers, the audience shifting in their seats.

She waited. The violin and bow hung loosely from her relaxed right hand. She thought of all the entrances, all the stages, all her years of Stradivarius. Her arm began to tingle, like the pinprick feeling of warm blood rushing under cold skin. All her years of Stradivarius. All the music she had played, always with the correct amount of passion and control. All the music that she had been in those moments suddenly swelled in her; she heard every note, felt every beat, tasted every breath that had ever taken her through a complicated phrase. She felt dizzy. A pulse pounded in her stomach. Her hand, and the violin, began to tremble.

The ASM cued her entrance.

She took the stage, head shaking. The audience rumbled. She found her place in the hot light, and when she breathed the audience breathed with her. The Judges nodded. She lifted the violin. It felt warm against her neck. One of the Judges asked, "Are you ready?" and she smiled. "Yes," she said, and white heat shot through her; "yes," she said again, and felt a hum inside her like cricketsong in her bones; and *yes*, she thought, and the door that had been shut so tight within her burst open, and the music battered through, spinning inside every part of her like a dervish, like a whirlwind, like a storm on the ocean that took the tidewater out and spit it back in giant surges. The music in her exulted and laughed and wept and reached out, farther, farther, until she wondered why everyone in the room did not stop, look, point, dance, run. It poured out sweet and strong through her heart and head and hands into the wood and gut of the violin that was her second voice, and her song was *yes* and *yes* and *yes* in a shout and a whisper and a pure, high cry. She played. She saw Monitors stumbling down the aisles and out from backstage, slowly at first and then fast, faster, toward her with outstretched hands and outraged eyes. She saw men and women in the audience rise to their feet, mouths and eyes and ears open, and *they hear*, she thought as the Monitors brought her down, *they hear* as her violin hit the floor and snapped in two with a wail, *they hear* as her arms were pinned behind her, *they hear*, and she smiled. Her hands were empty. She was full of music.

And Salome Danced

They're the best part, auditions: the last chance to hold in my mind the play as it should be. The uncast actors are easiest to direct; empty stages offer no barriers. Everything is clear, uncomplicated by living people and their inability to be what is needed.

"What I need," I say to my stage manager, "is a woman who can work on her feet."

"Hmm," says Lucky helpfully. She won't waste words on anything so obvious. Our play is *Salome*, subtitled *Identity and Desire*. Salome has to dance worth killing for.

The sense I have, in those best, sweet moments, is that I do not so much envision the play as experience it in some sort of multidimensional *gestalt*. I *feel* Salome's pride and the terrible control of her body's rhythms; Herod's twitchy groin and his guilt and his unspoken love for John; John's relentless patience, and his fear. The words of the script sometimes seize me as if bypassing vision, burrowing from page into skin, pushing blood and nerve to the bursting limit on the journey to my brain. The best theatre lives inside. I'll spend weeks trying to feed the sensation and the bloodsurge into the actors, but... But I can't do their job. But they can't read my mind. And people wonder why we drink

Lucky snorts at me when I tell her these things: if it isn't a tech cue or a blocking note, it has nothing to do with the real play as far as she's concerned. She doesn't understand that for me the play is best before it is real, when it is still only mine.

"Nine sharp," she says now. "Time to start. Some of them have already been out there long enough to turn green." She smiles; her private joke.

"Let's go," I say, my part of the ritual; and then I have to do it, have to let go. I sit forward over the script in my usual eighth row seat; Lucky takes her clipboard and her favorite red pen, the one she's had since *Cloud Nine*, up the aisle. She pushes open the lobby door and the sound of voices rolls through, cuts off. All of them out there, wanting in. I feel in my gut their tense waiting silence as Lucky calls the first actor's name.

They're hard on everyone, auditions. Actors bare their throats. Directors make instinctive leaps of faith about what an actor could or might or must do in this or that role, with this or that partner. It's kaleidoscopic, religious, it's violent and subjective. It's like soldiers fighting each other just to see who gets to go to war. Everyone gets bloody, right from the start.

Forty minutes before a late lunch break, when my blood sugar is at its lowest point, Lucky comes back with

the next resume and headshot and the first raised eye-brow of the day. The eyebrow, the snort, the flared nos-tril, the slight nod are Lucky's only comments on actors. They are minimal and emphatic.

Behind her walks John the Baptist. He calls himself Joe Something-or-other, but he's John straight out of my head. Dark red hair. The kind of body that muscles up long and compact, strong and lean. He moves well, con-fident but controlled. When he's on stage he even stands like a goddamn prophet. And his eyes are John's eyes: deep blue like deep sea. He wears baggy khaki trou-sers, a loose, untucked white shirt, high top sneakers, a Greek fisherman's cap. His voice is clear, a half-tone lighter than many people expect in a man: perfect.

The monologue is good, too. Lucky shifts in her seat next to me. We exchange a look, and I see that her pu-pils are wide.

"Is he worth dancing for, then?"

She squirms, all the answer I really need. I look at the resume again. Joe Sand. He stands calmly on stage. Then he moves very slightly, a shifting of weight, a leaning in toward Lucky. While he does it, he looks right at her, watching her eyes for that uncontrollable pupil response. He smiles. Then he tries it with me. *Aha*, I think, *surprise, little actor.*

"Callbacks are Tuesday and Wednesday nights," I say neutrally. "We'll let you know."

He steps off the stage. He is half in shadow when he asks, "Do you have Salome yet?"

"No precasting," Lucky says.

"I know someone you'd like," he says, and even though I can't quite see him I know he is talking to me.

Without the visual cue of his face, the voice has become transgendered, the body shape ambiguous.

"Any more at home like you, Joe?" I must really need my lunch.

"Whatever you need," he says, and moves past me, past Lucky, up the aisle. Suddenly, I'm ravenously hungry. Four more actors between me and the break, and I know already that I won't remember any of them longer than it takes for Lucky to close the doors behind them.

The next day is better. By late afternoon I have seen quite a few good actors, men and women, and Lucky has started a callback list.

"How many left?" I ask, coming back from the bathroom, rubbing the back of my neck with one hand and my waist with the other. I need a good stretch, some sweaty muscle-heating exercise, a hot bath. I need Salome.

Lucky is frowning at a paper in her hand. "Why is Joe Sand on this list?"

"God, Lucky, I want him for callbacks, that's why."

"No, this sheet is today's auditions."

I read over her shoulder. *Jo Sand.* "Dunno. Let's go on to the next one, maybe we can actually get back on schedule."

When I next hear Lucky's voice, after she has been up to the lobby to bring in the next actor, I know that something is terribly wrong.

"Mars... Mars..."

By this time I have stood and turned and I can see for myself what she is not able to tell me.

"Jo Sand," I say.

"Hello again," she says. The voice is the same; *she* is the same, and utterly different. She wears the white shirt tucked into the khaki pants this time, pulled softly across her breasts. Soft black shoes, like slippers, that make no noise when she moves. No cap today, that red hair thick, brilliant above the planes of her face. Her eyes are Salome's eyes: deep blue like deep desire. She is as I imagined her. When she leans slightly toward me, she watches my eyes and then smiles. Her smell goes straight up my nose and punches into some ancient place deep in my brain.

We stand like that for a long moment, the three of us. I don't know what to say. I don't have the right words for conversation with the surreal except when it's inside my head. I don't know what to do when it walks down my aisle and shows me its teeth.

"I want you to see that I can be versatile," Jo says.

The air in our small circle has become warm and sticky. My eyes feel slightly crossed, my mind is slipping gears. *I won't ask, I will not ask...* It's as if I were trying to bring her into focus through 3-D glasses; trying to make two separate images overlay. It makes me seasick. I wonder if Lucky is having the same trouble, and then I see that she has simply removed herself in some internal way. She doesn't see Jo look at me with those primary eyes.

But I see: and suddenly I feel wild, electric, that direct-brain connection that makes my nerves stand straight under my skin. *Be careful what you ask for, Mars.* "I don't guess you really need to do another monologue," I tell her. Lucky is still slack-jawed with shock.

Jo smiles again.

Someone else is talking with my voice. "Lucky will schedule you for callbacks." Beside me, Lucky jerks at the sound of her name. Jo turns to her. Her focus is complete. Her whole body says, *I am waiting.* I want her on stage. I want to see her like that, waiting for John's head on a platter.

"Mars, what..." Lucky swallows, tries again. She speaks without looking at the woman standing next to her. "Do you want... oh, shit. What part are you reading this person for in callbacks, goddamn it anyway." I haven't seen her this confused since her mother's boyfriend made a pass at her years ago, one Thanksgiving, his hand hidden behind the turkey platter at the buffet. Confusion makes Lucky fragile and brings her close to tears.

Jo looks at me, still waiting. Yesterday I saw John the Baptist: I remember how he made Lucky's eyebrow quirk and I can imagine the rehearsals; how he might sit close to her, bring her coffee, volunteer to help her set props. She'd be a wreck in one week and useless in two. And today how easy it is to see Salome, who waits so well and moves with such purpose. I should send this Jo away, but I won't: I need a predator for Salome; I can't do a play about desire without someone who knows the taste of blood.

"Wear a skirt," I say to Jo. "I'll need to see you dance." Lucky closes her eyes.

Somehow we manage the rest of the auditions, make the first cut, organize the callback list. There are very few actors I want to see again. When we meet for callbacks, I bring them all in and sit them in a clump at the rear of the house, where I can see them when I want to and ignore them otherwise. But always I am conscious of Jo. I read her with the actors that I think will work best in other roles. She is flexible, adapting herself to their different styles, giving them what they need to make the scene work. She's responsive to direction. She listens well. I can't find anything wrong with her.

Then it is time for the dance. There are three women I want to see, and I put them all on stage together. "Salome's dance is the most important scene in the play. It's a crisis point for every character. Everyone has something essential invested in it. It has to carry a lot of weight."

"What are you looking for?" one of the women asks. She has long dark hair and good arms.

"Power," I answer, and beside her Jo's head comes up like a pointing dog's, her nostrils flared with some rich scent. I pretend not to see. "Her dance is about power over feelings and lives. There's more, but power's the foundation, and that's what I need to see."

The woman who asked nods her head and looks down, chewing the skin off her upper lip. I turn away to give them a moment for this new information to sink in; looking out into the house, I see the other actors sitting forward in their seats, and I know they are wondering who it will be, and whether they could work with her, and what they would do in her place.

I turn back. "I want you all to dance together up here. Use the space any way you like. Take a minute to warm up and start whenever you're ready."

I can see the moment that they realize, *ohmigod no music, how can we dance without, goddamn all directors anyway*. But I want to see their interpretation of power, not music. If they don't have it in them to dance silent in front of strangers, if they can't compete, if they can't pull all my attention and keep it, then they can't give me what I need. Salome wouldn't hesitate.

The dark haired woman shrugs, stretches her arms out and down toward her toes. The third woman slowly begins to rock her hips; her arms rise swaying in the cliche of eastern emerald-in-the-navel bellydance. She moves as if embarrassed, and I don't blame her. The dark-haired woman stalls for another moment and then launches into a jerky jazz step with a strangely syncopated beat. I can almost hear her humming her favorite song under her breath; her head tilts up and to the right and she moves in her own world, to her own sound. That's not right, either. I realize that I'm hoping one of them will be what I need, so that I do not have to see Jo dance.

And where is Jo? There, at stage right, watching the other two women, comfortable in her stillness. Then she slides gradually into motion, steps slowly across the stage and stops three feet from the bellydancer, whose stumbling rhythm slows and then breaks as Jo stands, still, watching. Jo looks her straight in the eye, and just as the other woman begins to drop her gaze, Jo suddenly whirls, throwing herself around so quickly that for an instant it's as if her head is facing the opposite direction from her body. It is a nauseating moment, and it's followed by a total body shrug, a shaking off, that is both contemptuous and intently erotic. Now she is facing the house, facing the other actors, facing Lucky, facing me: now she shows us what she can do. Her dance says, *This is what I am, that you can never be; see my body move as it will never move with yours.* She stoops for an imaginary platter, and from the triumph in her step I begin to see the bloody prize. The curve of her arm shows me the filmed eye and the lolling tongue; the movement of her breast and belly describe for me the wreckage of the neck, its trailing cords; her feet draw pictures in the splashed gore as she swirls and turns and snaps her arm out like a discus thrower, tossing the invisible trophy straight at me. When I realize that I have raised a hand to catch it, I know that I have to have her, no matter what she is. Have to have her for the play. Have to have her.

When the actors are gone, Lucky and I go over the list. We do not discuss Salome. Lucky has already set the other two women's resumes aside.

Before we leave: "God, she was amazing. She'll be great, Mars. I'm really glad it turned out this way, you know, that she decided to drop that crossdressing stuff."

"Mmm."

"It really gave me a start, seeing her that day. She was so convincing as a man. I thought… well, nothing. It was stupid."

"It wasn't stupid."

"You didn't seem surprised—did you know that first time when he… when she came in that she wasn't…? Why didn't you say?"

"If I'm looking at someone who can play John, I don't really care how they pee or whether they shave under their chins. Gender's not important."

"It is if you think you might want to go to bed with it."

"Mmm," I say again. What I cannot tell Lucky is that all along I have been in some kind of shock; like walking through swamp mud, where the world is warm silkywet but you are afraid to look down for fear of what might be swimming with you in the murk. I know this is not a game: Joe was a man when he came in and a woman when she came back. I look at our cast list, and I know that something impossible and dangerous is trying to happen; but all I really see is that suddenly my play—the one inside me—is possible. She'll blow a hole through every seat in the house. She'll burst their brains.

※

Three weeks into rehearsal, Lucky has unremembered enough to start sharing coffee and head-together conferences with Jo during breaks. The other actors accept Jo as someone they can't believe they never heard of before, a comrade in the art wars. We are such a happy group; we give great ensemble.

Lance, who plays Herod, regards Jo as some kind of wood sprite, brilliant and fey. He is myopic about her to the point that if she turned into an anaconda, he would stroke her head while she wrapped herself around him. Lance takes a lot of kidding about his name, especially from his boyfriends. During our early rehearsals, he discovered a very effective combination of obsession and revulsion in Herod: as if he would like to eat Salome alive and then throw her up again, a sort of sexual bulimia.

Susan plays Herodias; Salome's mother, Herod's second wife, his brother's widow. She makes complicated seem simple. She works well with Lance, giving him a strong partner who nevertheless dims in comparison to her flaming daughter, a constant reminder to Herod of the destruction that lurks just on the other side of a single *yes* to this stepdaughter/niece/demonchild who dances in his fantasies. Susan watches Jo so disinterestedly that it has taken me most of this time to see how she has imitated and matured the arrogance that Jo brings to the stage. She is a tall black woman, soft muscle where Jo is hard: nothing like Jo, but she has become Salome's mother.

And John the Baptist, whose real name is Frank and who is nothing like Joe: I'm not sure I could have cast him if he had come to the audition with red hair, but his is black this season, Irish black for the O'Neill repertory production he just finished. Lucky says he has "Jesus feet." Frankie's a method actor, disappointed that he doesn't have any sense memory references for decapitation. "I know it happens offstage," he says earnestly, at least once a week. "But it needs to be there right from the start. I want them to think about it every scene with her." *Them* is always the audience. *Her* is always Jo. Offstage, he looks at her the way a child looks at a harvest moon.

Three weeks is long enough for us all to become comfortable with the process but not with the results: the discoveries the actors made in the first two weeks refuse to gel, refuse to reinvent themselves. It's a frustrating phase. We're all tense but trying not to show it, trying not to undermine anyone else's efforts. It's hard for the actors, who genuinely want to support each other but don't really want to see someone else break through first. Too scary: no one wants to be left behind. So they give themselves up to me. Between us is so much deliberate vulnerability, control, desire to please; so much of the stuff that sex is made of. Working with my actors is like handling bolts of cloth: they each have a texture, a tension. Lance is brocade and plush; Susan is smooth velvet, subtle to the touch; Frankie is spun wool, warm and indefinably tough. And Jo: Jo is raw silk and razorblades, so fine that you don't feel the cut.

So we're all tense; except for Jo. Oh, she talks, but she's not worried; she's waiting for something, and I am beginning to turn those audition days over in my memory, sucking the taste from the bones of those encounters and wondering what it was that danced with me in those early rounds, what I have invited in.

And a peculiar thing begins: as I grow more disturbed, Jo's work becomes better and better. In those moments when I suddenly see myself as the trainer with my head in the mouth of the beast, when I slip and show that my hand is sweaty on the leash—in those moments her work is so pungent, so ripe that Jo the world-shaker disappears, and the living Salome looks up from the cut-off t-shirt, flexes her thigh muscles under the carelessly torn jeans. We have more and more of Salome every rehearsal.

On Friday nights I bring a cooler of Corona and a bag of limes for whoever wants to share them. This Friday everyone stays. We sit silent for the first cold green-gold swallows. Lance settles back into Herod's large throne. I straddle a folding chair and rest my arms along the back, bottle loose in one hand. Lucky and the other actors settle on the platforms that break the stage into playing areas.

It starts with the actors talking, as they always do, about work. Lance has played another Herod, years ago, in *Jesus Christ Superstar*, and he wants to tell us how different that was.

"I'd like to do *Superstar*," Jo says. It sounds like an idle remark. She is leaning back with her elbows propped against the rise of a platform, her breasts pushing gently against the fabric of her shirt as she raises her bottle to her mouth. I look away because I do not want to watch her drink, don't want to see her throat work as the liquid goes down.

Lance considers a moment. "I think you'd be great, sweetheart," he says, "But Salome to Mary Magdalene is a pretty big stretch. Acid to apple juice. Wouldn't you at least like to play a semi-normal character in between, work up to it a little?"

Jo snorts. "I'm not interested in Magdalene. I'll play Judas."

Lance whoops, Frankie grins, and even the imperturbable Susan smiles. "Well, why not?" Lance says. "Why shouldn't she play Judas if she wants to?"

"She's a girl," Frankie says, and shrugs.

Susan sits up. "Why shouldn't she have the part if she can do the work?"

Frankie gulps his beer and wipes his mouth. "Why should any director hire a woman to play a man when they can get a real man to do it?"

"What do you think, Mars?" The voice is Jo's. It startles me. I have been enjoying the conversation so much that I have forgotten the danger in relaxing around Jo or anything that interests her. I look at her now, still sprawled back against the platform with an inch of golden beer in the bottle beside her. She has been enjoying herself, too. I'm not sure where this is going, what the safe answer is. I remember saying to Lucky, *Gender's not important.*

"Gender's not important, isn't that right, Mars?"

Lucky told her about it. But I know Lucky didn't. She didn't have to.

"That's right," I say, and I know from Jo's smile that my voice is not as controlled as it should be. Even so, I'm not prepared for what happens next: a jumble of pictures in my head, images of dancing in a place so dark that I cannot tell if I am moving with men or women, images of streets filled with androgynous people and people whose gender-blurring surpasses androgyny and leaps into the realm of performance. Women dressed as men making love to men; men dressed as women hesitating in front of public bathroom doors; women in high heels and pearls with biceps so large that they split the expensive silk shirts. And the central image, the real point: Jo, naked, obviously female, slick with sweat, moving under me and over me, Jo making love to me until I gasp and then she begins to change, to change, until it is Joe with me, Joe on me—and I open my mouth to shout my absolute, instinctive refusal—and I remember Lucky saying *It is if you think you might want to sleep with it*— and the movie breaks in my head and I am back with the others. No one has noticed that I've been assaulted, turned inside out. They're still talking about it: "Just imagine the difference in all the relationships if Judas were a woman," Susan says earnestly to Frankie. "It would change everything!" Jo smiles at me and swallows the last of her beer.

The next rehearsal I feel fragile, as if I must walk carefully to keep from breaking myself. I have to rest often.

I am running a scene with Frankie and Lance when I notice Lucky offstage, talking earnestly to Jo. Jo puts one hand up, interrupts her, smiles, speaks, and they both turn to look at me. Lucky suddenly blushes. She walks quickly away from Jo, swerves to avoid me. Jo's smile is bigger. Her work in the next scene is particularly fine and full.

"What did she say to you, Luck?" I ask her as we are closing the house for the evening.

"Nothing," Lucky mumbles.

"Come on."

"Okay, fine. She wanted to know if you ever slept with your actors, okay?"

I know somehow that it's not entirely true: I can hear Jo's voice very clearly, saying to Lucky, *So does Mars ever fuck the leading lady?* while she smiles that catlick smile. Jo has the gift of putting pictures into people's heads, and I believe Lucky got a mindful. That's what really sickens me, the idea that Lucky now has an image behind her eyes of what I'm like... no, of what Jo wants her to think I'm like. God knows. I don't want to look at her.

"Did you get my message?" Jo says to me the next evening, when she finally catches me alone in the wings during a break from rehearsal. She has been watching me all night. Lucky won't talk to her.

"I'm not in the script."

"Everybody's in the script."

"Look, I don't get involved with actors. It's too complicated, it's messy. I don't do it."

"Make an exception."

Lucky comes up behind Jo. Whatever the look is on my face, it gets a scowl from her. "Break's over," she says succinctly, turning away from us even before the words are completely out, halfway across the stage before I think to try to keep her with me.

"Let's get back to work, Jo."

"Make a fucking exception."

I don't like being pushed by actors, and there's something else, too, but I don't want to think about it now, I just want Jo off my back, so I give her the director voice, the vocal whip. "Save it for the stage. You want to impress me, get out there and do your fucking job."

She doesn't answer; her silence makes a cold, high-altitude circle around us. When she moves, it's like a snake uncoiling, and then her hand is around my wrist. She's *strong*. When I look down, I see that her hand is changing: the bones thicken under the flesh, the muscles rearrange themselves subtly, and it's Joe's hand on Jo's arm, Joe's hand on mine. "Don't make me angry, Mars," and the voice is genderless and buzzes like a snake. There is no one here to help me, I can't see Lucky,

I'm all alone with this hindbrain thing that wants to come out and play with me. Jo's smile is by now almost too big for her face. *Just another actor*, I think crazily, *they're all monsters anyway*.

"What are you?" I am shaking.

"Whatever you need, Mars. Whatever you need. Every director's dream. At the moment, I'm Salome, right down to the bone. I'm what you asked for."

"I didn't ask for this. I don't want this."

"You wanted Salome, and now you've got her. The power, the sex, the hunger, the need, the wanting, it's all here."

"It's a play. It's just... it's a play, for chrissake."

"It's real for you." That hand is still locked around my wrist; the other hand, the soft small hand, reaches up to the center of my chest where my heart tries to skitter away from her touch. "I saw it, that first audition. I came to play John the Baptist, I saw the way Lucky looked at me, and I was going to give her something to remember... but your wanting was so strong, so complex. It's delicious, Mars. It tastes like spice and wine and sweat. The play in your head is more real to you than anything, isn't it, more real than your days of bright sun, your friends, your office transactions. I'm going to bring it right to you, into your world, into your life. I'll give you Salome. On stage, off stage, there doesn't have to be any difference. Isn't that what making love is, giving someone what they really want?"

She's still smiling that awful smile, and I can't tell whether she is talking about love because she really means it or because she knows it makes my stomach turn over. Or maybe both.

"Get out of here. Out of here, right now." I am shaking.

"You don't mean that, sweet. If you did, I'd already be gone."

"I'll cancel the show."

She doesn't answer: she looks at me and then, *phht*, I am seeing the stage from the audience perspective, watching Herod and Herodias quarrel and cry and struggle to protect their love, watching John's patient fear as Herod's resolve slips away: watching Salome dance. When she dances, she brings us all with her, the whole audience living inside her skin for those moments. We all whirl and reach and bend, we all promise, we all twist away. We all tempt. We all rage. We stuff ourselves down Herod's throat until he chokes on us. And then we are all suddenly back in our own bodies and we roar until our throats hurt and our voices rasp. All the things that I have felt about this play, she will make them feel. What I am will be in them. What I have inside me will bring them to their feet and leave them full and aching. Oh god, it makes me weep, and then I am back with her, she still holds me with that monster hand, and all I can do is cry with wanting so badly what she can give me.

Her eyes are too wide, too round, too pleased. "Oh," she says, still gently, "It's okay. You'll enjoy most of it, I promise." And she's gone, sauntering onstage, calling out something to Lance, and her upstage hand is still too big, still wrong. She lets it caress her thigh once before she turns it back into the Jo hand. I've never seen anything more obscene. I have to take a minute to dry my eyes, cool my face. I feel a small, hollow place somewhere deep, as if Jo reached inside and found something she liked enough to take for herself. She's there now, just onstage, ready to dance, that small piece of me humming in her veins. How much more richness do I have within me? How long will it take to eat me, bit by bit? She raises her arms now and smiles, already tasting. Already well fed.

City Life

Charlie was dancing on the edge of the grave the day he met her. She walked to him across the lazy green of the cemetery, the fragrance of the gardenias pinned in her hair mingling with the smell of fresh-turned earth.

"What are you doing?" she asked.

He considered the question. The toe of his shoe thumped a clod of fresh dirt into the grave.

"It was supposed to be the jig," he said finally, "but I can't lift my knees high enough anymore." Then he cried.

When he stopped wailing, he found himself caught up in the arms and eyes and hair of the woman. Gardenias tickled his nose, their petals brown and curling now. He felt warm and pleasantly drained and suddenly shy, and he used his trembling arms to set himself away from her.

"I'm sorry," he said finally. "It's just that I'm sick." At the edge of his vision, blue and red birds swooped and cackled amid the headstones.

"You're fine," she said, and smiled. Charlie sat back on his heels in the dirt and swiped one hand across his nose, thinking about not seeing his fortieth birthday, thinking that she did not understand.

"I understand perfectly," she said. He was shocked; his heart slammed a quick three-two beat against his ribs. The woman stood up and smiled again and went away across the level plots where graves would someday be. Behind Charlie a bird stopped singing.

⚘

A few days later he stepped from the dark doorway of the clinic into the downtown sun, cried-out and flying high and determined to find her again, to thank her and ask her *how*.

An errant breeze bounced among the pockets and nooks of the buildings on the Chicago street. Up the block he could see the last of the afternoon's crowds crossing against the traffic light. He looked the other way and saw motion, something bobbing and weaving down the sidewalk. Dust-devil, he thought at first, haven't seen one of those in a long time.

He squinted into the afternoon light. The dust-devil was wearing a rubber raincoat.

The dust-devil was a woman carrying hard years in her face and on her back. Her stained khaki pants were held up by a piece of rope, one end of which was jerked and tugged in the clenching and unclenching of a pitted hand. It looked as if she were pulling herself forward down the street by the rope; Charlie was sure that she would pull too hard and either pitch right over or yank off her rancid trousers, to the horror of passers-by. The image had him smiling when the dust-devil passed him in a roiling of grit and newspaper fragments, orange peels

and grey vacuum. Voices leaked from the plug that connected her left ear to the battered transistor radio sticking
out of the raincoat pocket.

Charlie thought that since he had been caught smiling
he might as well go for broke. He nodded. "Hi," he said.

The old woman's jaw was purple-shadowed, and her
eyes were bruised. When she grinned, Charlie saw lumps
of black tissue on the inside of her mouth. "Sick," the old
woman said wetly.

"Oh, no," Charlie replied. "I feel fine..." but she had
already gone swirling up the street. Charlie heard the
faint sounds of a train pulling into a station somewhere
under his feet. Its vibrations blew a gust of hot air out of a
sidewalk grate, rattling a strip of newspaper that had fall-
en off the old woman. It skittered past Charlie's feet. All
he could read of the headline was "Sears Tower Window
Falls Fifty-Seven Floors To Street."

On his way home, he saw the woman from the grave-
yard on the train.

He pushed his way through two and a half crowded
Elevated train cars to reach her, and she only looked at
him with a sort of wary puzzlement and said, "I'm afraid
you must be mistaken. I don't know what you're talking
about." But Charlie knew that he had not misremembered
her eyes, or the long bark-brown hair he had cried into.
And, of course, the gardenias.

She ignored his protests and his pleadings and left
him at the Wilson Avenue station. "Do you live around
here?" he asked frantically as the El doors opened and rid-
ers began to edge in and out of the cars.

"No," she replied, and stepped out.

"Wait!" he called. She half-turned towards him, while the people-stream split around her on the platform.

"At least tell me your name?" he asked.

"Magdalena," she said, and then Charlie saw her smile become subtly unfocused, and her face and neck flushed. A haggard, hunched woman brushing past stopped, put one hand to a sweat-slicked temple, and slowly straightened up. She looked around her in wonderment and a little fear as Magdalena, remote and serene, pushed open the swinging doors of the station staircase and went through.

Charlie went to his editor the next day. Max pumped Charlie's arm up and down and back-thumped and atta-boyed him so much that he was ready to back out of the office until he saw Max's eyes wet behind his glasses. Then it was too late; Charlie was already hooked by his own sense of responsibility at finding himself the target of someone else's concern. It was a relief when Max rubbed his nose and reached behind his computer for the bottle of apricot brandy that he reserved for special occasions. Charlie thought he would just as soon not have ever been anybody's special occasion again if it meant another round of Max's damn apricot brandy.

They drank a silent toast from stiff, flat-bottomed paper cups that Max had taken from the water fountain years earlier. He washed them meticulously in the bathroom after every use. Charlie tried to sip without letting his lips touch the frayed edges of the cup.

Max shook his head. "I can't believe it," he said again. "*Total* recovery? Are they sure? How could it... I mean, I'm glad, but how could something like this happen?"

"I want to talk to you about that," Charlie said.

⚓

But a part of him had known even before he went to Max how he would be treated: kindly and gently, because Max respected him enough to hide any disbelief. Charlie sat at his desk in the front office outlining his overdue article on delays in the city's schedule of street repairs, and answering the phone because the receptionist had not yet come back from lunch. He was grateful in a slightly annoyed way that the phones kept him busy; every time he started typing out the notes for his article, he would remember one of Max's comments. After all, Charlie, this is the *Rogers Park Weekly News*, not the *Chicago Tribune*. Or the *Enquirer*. After all, Charlie, you have been under a lot of stress. Do you want some time off? No, really, it would be okay. After all, Charlie, if we start printing stories about mystic healers then we'll have to let Mrs. Morton submit her piece on the UFO she saw in the parking lot of the bank over on Clark Street.

When he found himself typing "after all, Charlie" into his notes on the street repair article, he hit the keys that would save the file on the computer and jerked himself out of his chair and over to the door of Max's office to say he was going to lunch. Max just gave him what Charlie always thought of as The Look, the raised eyebrow over the top of the tortoise-shell frames.

On the way out the door he fumbled in the inside pocket of his jacket, looking for his sunglasses. They caught on the jacket lining and he pulled too hard, stumbled down the front stairs of the building, and caught himself with his left hand on the wooden banister. A splinter needled hot and jagged into the pad of flesh at the top of his palm just below the index finger.

He swore savagely, trying to cover splinters and condescending bosses and all the crazy women in the world in one series of vicious words. He was so caught up that he did not see the shadow that spiraled up behind him.

Before he heard the voice he smelled the breath, rotted breath, and in it the carcasses of dead cats in dumpsters, diesel fumes from the trucks that circle in and out of loading docks at grocery stores, excreta caked in the grooves of rubber Welcome mats. Pigeons' wings whirred in the wind of that voice, and car tires squealed. The voice slid into his ear as cold and implacable as the IV needle in the arm of the policeman lying in the back of the ambulance that went screaming past at the precise moment that Charlie turned and found himself looking into the mouth of the dust-devil woman.

He jolted backward, and his stomach tried to push itself up through his throat. He felt as if all the air had been sucked from his lungs straight into the dust-devil's mouth. The old woman was taller and larger than Charlie remembered, and her mouth seemed somehow too big, too deep for her cracked and knobby face. Inside the mouth, dark things moved sluggishly across the leathery tongue. The mouth blew unspeakable things into Charlie's ear, into his brain, whirling the sounds around so that he couldn't understand what was happening. The voice numbed him.

And then the sky tilted crazy for a split-second, and Charlie realized that she was only an old woman, nothing more, an old raggedy crazy woman nodding her head, mumbling and chuckling in a sing-song monologue about the stock prices and barometric readings and traffic reports that poured into her ear through the square transistor AM radio that Charlie had noticed before in her coat pocket.

"Sick," she said suddenly and clearly through the mush of her mutterings. She tilted her head and looked at Charlie sidewise, the way a bird might, blinking quickly. A flap of skin fell away from the exposed side of her neck, just peeled down while Charlie watched. It hung limp against the collar of her coat. Small flecks of older dead skin speckled her shoulders and sleeves.

Christ, Charlie thought, she means that *she's* sick. The old woman lurched away, her unlaced canvas shoes scuffling on the city pavement.

From down the street came a series of sharp cracks that echoed like gunshot ricochets. When Charlie got there, he found that a section of sidewalk, part of the street repair project, had collapsed into the sewer below, falling away from under the feet of three children playing with a neighbor's dog. The dog was not hurt at all, only because it landed on top of the children and the ragged chunks of concrete.

He sat on his favorite stool, the second-to-last stool at Palley's bar. It was the only Irish bar he knew with a Pakistani bartender. Ahmal always served Charlie call brands at house prices because he was convinced that Charlie was a hot reporter for the *Tribune*. He would even say sometimes, "Hey, Charlie, I see your article in the paper today, very nice." Usually Charlie would smile or nod, and say a rueful thanks, having learned that it was useless to protest. Today he could only look away and make motions for another drink. He carried a copy of the paper folded to the headline, "Two Children Killed In Street Accident." It was his first *Tribune* byline.

The whiskey pooled in the bottom of his glass, in the bottom of his throat, and dropped into the lowest part of his stomach. The splinter in his palm, still raw, throbbed with each pulse-surge. At each beat of blood through his hand he thought of the dust-devil woman. He felt her breath again on the back of his neck, he remembered what he had not allowed himself to hear when that voice had slid like a snail into his ear, that dispassionate hollow voice that had said *The woman, the woman, show me, bring me the woman, bring me her light, bring me her heart.* The whiskey turned to points of ice in his stomach, and at each chill that rippled through his ribs and arms, that made his fingers shake, Charlie thought of Magdalena.

⚘

He saw her again, this time from a distance. He was walking toward the hospital where the one surviving child from the sidewalk collapse was recovering. He had an appointment to talk further with the child's mother, and he was dreading it. His head hurt, and he felt as if someone had hung a brick around his neck. Then a block away he saw Magdalena walking down the wide stairs from the hospital to the street. "Hey," he shouted, "Miss! Magdalena! Please!"

She turned and looked at him, and it was obvious she recognized him from the train, and that she was afraid. By the time he reached the corner, she was gone, hidden among the crowd.

He went into the hospital and found the injured child giggling, walking, whole.

He tried for several days to find her, in spite of Max's growing worry and impatience, which he expressed in midnight phone calls and pointed references to unemployment. Charlie walked the streets of the Loop and waited for hours in the major Elevated train stations, the ones where she might stop to change trains or catch a bus. Once he thought he saw a woman of browns and creams and softness, but it was not her. Yet he knew she was close. He saw it in the crowds that spilled around him from the subways and elevators and revolving doors of the city. Some of the faces were especially smooth and taut, the bodies full of the same almost palpable good health and vitality that Charlie had felt after his brush with her. When he looked at those people, he saw something at the back of their eyes that told him they had met a mystery. He knew that although he could not see Magdalena, he had found her reflected in the eyes of the city.

More than once he saw other things, things that disturbed him. Sometimes the sun would flash off a grey rubber sleeve in the crowd. And in the past few days, at times, the air around him would become cold and still, and tin cans and sandwich crusts would suddenly ricket along the ground, as if being pulled towards a central point that started to become a whirling, spiraling mass of smoky air. Then he would leave wherever he was. He would take the next train or bus, or he would run in furious zigzag patterns through the streets until his legs hurt. He did that if he felt even the slightest hint of a whirlwind coming on; he had stayed once long enough to see a pair of rheumy eyes blink open in the middle of a sodden mass of chewed donuts and cigarette butts, and to smell the sharp tang of ozone.

In those moments, leaning against a building or a railing to catch his breath, wiping the fear-sweat from the hollow of his neck, Charlie would know that he was insane. Once he stopped to rest on a park bench, but when he sat down one iron leg of the bench twisted and the wooden seat tilted him off onto the grass. He sat on the ground and shook for twenty minutes before he could get up again. He knew he could never tell anyone, not even Max, that he was seeing and doing these things. Except he thought that maybe he could tell Magdalena, maybe she would understand. And he thought of her as he'd seen her in the cemetery and on the train, vibrant but somehow fragile, and he remembered her outside the hospital, so frightened. She glowed in his mind.

～

"You have to come back to work," Max said on the phone that night. "There is so much going on in this city right now that no one can keep up with it all. We're getting calls from the *Trib* and the *Sun-Times* for neighborhood reports. I need you right now."

Charlie sat slumped in a crooked armchair, half asleep with the late-summer, late-night breeze scratching against his bare feet and the back of his collar. He propped the phone receiver on his shoulder and leaned his head against it. "What are you talking about, Max?" He yawned.

"Where the hell have you been, Ace? If you'd been doing your damn job this past couple of days you would have heard about little things like the whole damn city falling apart."

"C'mon, Max," Charlie said. The movement of leafy branches outside the window cast hypnotic shadows on his wall. "Don't give me a line like that just to get me back in the office. Look, I'm sorry about this week. I know I haven't been… Maybe I am going crazy, I think I must be, but I just have to do this. Something really strange is going on, and I can't explain it, and I don't expect you to understand, but I've got to follow it. So don't run this on me."

A hard noise rocked his head back from the phone receiver. Whoops, he thought, Max never starts slamming things around on his desk unless he's ready to blow.

"Jesus Christ, Charlie!"

Here it comes, Charlie thought.

"What is with you? I know that you gotta do whatever it is that you've been doing lately and I know that you're gonna do it whether I understand or not, and you should sure as hell know that I would never ask you to drop something important to you even if it is crazy, just because I want you to cover another sighting of Martians at the Citicorp Bank. Now are you gonna get off your high horse and listen to me, or are we going to end this conversation?"

Charlie sat up in the chair with his elbows propped on his knees. There was a hole starting in the thigh of his jeans. He picked at the loose threads and counted to ten in Chinese. It took all his concentration.

"Well?"

"You're right, Max," he said. "Okay. What's the story?"

And he listened while Max told him.

Sidewalks fell in and killed children, not just near him but in at least three other places. In one instance, near the Lincoln Park Zoo, the concrete caved in to a pit that belched hot, rotten-egg gases. Cornices crumbled from the edges of brownstones and office buildings in renovated neighborhoods. Fuel pumps toppled on their concrete islands, and gasoline ran in the gutters past curbs that powdered into gravel under the heels of old women. Fire escape staircases buckled, and shattering windows blinded janitors in the metal and glass towers downtown. The bleachers at Wrigley Field twisted and collapsed, and the scoreboard exploded and burned. The hospitals filled with the casualties of the city while paint peeled in confetti strips from the walls of the emergency rooms.

Max talked on. Charlie held himself still, feeling a fragile understanding of some connection, a causality like a Japanese origami bird that held them all in its folds; him and the old woman, Magdalena and the city. The sense of it escaped him.

He sat very quiet for a long time after he hung up the phone. The things he had heard left him with a reluctance to move, an itchy under-the-skin fear of this wonderful, muscular city where he had spent so much of his life and his energy.

He rubbed his forehead with the side of his hand, wincing when the skin pulled across the splinter. Damn thing should have festered out by now, he thought, and turned on a table lamp for a closer look.

His palm was swollen tight, puffed and tender where the splinter lay, with streaks of red spreading out from it. Infection.

~~~

When he left his apartment the next morning, great grey clouds were gathering to the east and creeping toward the city across the sluggish, leaded water of the lake.

He could not see the sun at all. He rode the El south toward the Loop. Some of the buildings seemed tilted at subtle, crazy angles against the skyline. Looking ahead made him nauseous. The train rocked over the crossties from station to station. The train and the stations were almost empty of people, and filled with debris: half-eaten baseball hotdogs, broken toys, paper bags.

Wind blew through the windows of the train and riffled open a newspaper by his foot. The breeze pushed the paper along the grimy floor and out the open door at one end of the car. The paper splayed out for a moment before it spun out into the air over the tracks, and he saw a headline, "House On South Side Drips Blood."

The train pulled into the Belmont station at the same time that another from the Ravenswood line slowed and curved in to an adjacent track. The doors slid apart with a hiss and a puff of scented air, gardenias, and Magdalena stepped out.

She looked like the earth: brown hair, well-water eyes, strong supple hands like saplings brushing across the wooden supports of the walls as she walked toward him. They met at the center of the platform, underneath the blue station sign. Dead and dying moths drifted down from the rafters over their heads.

Oh God, he thought, what if she runs away again?

"Magdalena?"

She looked at him. "Dancing the jig," she said. "I remember you now."

Relief flashed through him, followed immediately by worry. He looked over both shoulders, trying to twist his head to see in all directions at once. Half his mind thought how ridiculous he must look, and the other half wondered what the hell he would do if the air in front of him began to coalesce and whisper.

She stood calmly while he thought. A moth in her hair fluttered and then flew away.

He nodded at her. "We need to talk," he said, "but not here. Come back to my place."

"Which way do you live?"

He thought it was a strange question. "North," he answered, with a little squint and shake of his head. He took a step toward the stairs that would lead them over to the waiting northbound train.

"No," she said sharply, and put a hand up to stop him. Although she did not quite touch him, he felt the heat that pressed out of her palm.

"I have to go south," she said. She laughed, but it was a tiny, helpless sound. "I'm sorry," she said, "I can't even give you a good reason for it. But I feel like I need to go south. I need your help." She smiled. "I'm glad I found you."

Charlie snorted and shook his head. "You're glad you found me?" He grinned. "You have no idea how funny that is." He wanted to put his arms around her. His left hand burned with sickness.

"If you want to go south, we'll go south," he said, "but first let's go get something to eat. You look like you could use it, and I know I could."

"All right." For a moment she was another woman, an ordinary woman in a tan dress and brown hair and a happy grin. Just being near her made Charlie feel full of possibility.

He opened the street door with one hand and reached out to her with the other, the bandaged left hand.

"I can't touch you," she said. Something broke inside Charlie when he saw the genuine sorrow on her face.

"What do you mean? Why not?"

He followed her through the door. She moved carefully.

Shortly after, air began to curl and coil on the empty platform.

⚓

They sat in the luncheonette booth. Magdalena stared out the window at the people coming and going to cars and houses and neighborhood shops. Charlie drew circles on his napkin with the handle of his coffee spoon. Fresh drops of coffee spattered the stained tabletop.

"Why not?" he asked again.

"Because something bad will happen." She was near crying, and her voice shook in her throat.

He stared at her. "What do you mean, something bad? What bad? Don't you know what you did for me? If I hadn't met you that day I'd be busy dying right now."

He pressed the spoon handle so hard into the table that it bent. It surprised him. When he looked back up at her, they were both crying.

"You saved me," he said. "I just wanted to thank you. That's why I was looking for you, when I saw you on the train before, that was the only reason. I swear."

"I know." She made her look take the place of reaching for his hand. "I know that now. I'm sorry I ran away."

They drank their coffee in silence. It tasted horrible, but Charlie signaled for another cup.

"What is it?" he asked, when the hot steam was curling up from the cups and the waitress had left. "What do you think is going to happen?"

"Things are falling apart." She swallowed. "I think it's my fault."

"That's ridiculous. That's just plain dumb. You have a gift, Magdalena, not a disease."

She set her cup back in its saucer with rattling quickness, and the corners of her mouth twisted up. "Don't patronize me."

"I only meant…"

"Just shut up." She was talking low and fast and focused, her words so pointed and directed that he thought he should feel them going through his chest, through cartilage and lung tissue and muscle.

"You don't know anything about it. It's not a gift, and it's not even something I have. It's something that has me."

She put her hands up to her cheeks, cupped her face. He could tell from the way she spoke that she was bone-tired. "Mostly it seems like days and days of dreams, dreams about moving through the city and putting my hands on people, holding them, feeding them light. Making them well."

Charlie nodded. "That's what you did for me."

"But don't you see," she said, "at the same time I've been making all these people well, the city has been getting sicker and sicker?"

Charlie hunched his shoulders and sighed. "Cities don't get sick," he said as gently as he could. He held up his hand to cut off her interruption. "None of this crazy stuff is your fault. That's just your imagination."

She was looking into her coffee as he finished. She had stopped crying, but tear tracks still shone on her cheeks. Her fingers trembled on the handle of the cup.

"All right," she said. "Give me your hand."

"What do you mean?"

"Just like it sounds."

He felt reluctant to unwrap the bandage. His hand hurt, and he did not want to see it, but he put it onto the tabletop between them, palm up. It had gone red shading into purple, puffed and streaked.

She took his hand. He felt a burning, as if he had put his palm against the casing of a metal shed in the sun, or the hood of a car after a long trip. That was something recent, he thought, he didn't remember it from the grave-yard encounter. The splinter twisted, twitched slightly, then jerked sharp out of its cocoon of flesh. Magdalena brushed it onto the floor. The flowers in her hair curled, their edges crisp. Charlie watched the skin on his hand weave together into a new scar, its center soft and pink.

"That was a small one," Magdalena said. "I hope it doesn't cost too much to show you this."

He looked at her, puzzled, and was opening his mouth to speak when a thud from outside and crunching of met-al on metal jolted him. He bit his tongue, and the blood from the little injury ran down the back of his throat as he leaned past her to look out the window, as he saw the jeep that lay half-crushed under the yellow, sharp-edged weight of the traffic light that had fallen from its support over the center of the intersection. Two young men in White Sox caps pulled the driver from his seat; he held his forehead so that the top half of his face, which was cut down one side from hairline to ear, would not flap over into his eyes.

Charlie made it to the stalls of the men's room before he got sick.

Magdalena was still at the table when he got back. For a moment, rubbing out his mouth with a gritty paper towel in the washroom, he hoped that he would come out and find her gone. And yet something relaxed inside him when he saw her there, her head propped on one hand, turned away from the window and the confusion beyond it. He knew her strength, he had felt the power in her; but sitting over her cold coffee she looked as fragile as the flowers she wore. A space opened up within Charlie; he felt bigger somehow. He wanted to walk tall and slay dragons and all that nonsense for her for the rest of his life. And he would even take her guilt, if he had to and if he could.

He sat down beside her on the booth seat. She flinched, shifted apologetically. The healing heat poured out of her.

"It's okay," he said. "I don't even have a cavity, I promise. No scratches, no paper cuts, nothing."

She smiled a little, bowed her head. He thought she was trying not to cry again.

"I believe you," he said. "I'm sorry I didn't before. But it's still not your fault. You didn't mean to hurt anyone."

She was rubbing her eyes and sniffling into her crumpled napkin. "It doesn't matter," she said. "It doesn't matter what I meant to do, it's what I did. And it's getting so much worse. I'm responsible. I'm responsible for what just happened out there, that poor man's face, and the sidewalks and the rats and...and all those *people*," and she could not continue, she just leaned over onto his shoulder and wept.

He held her, much as she had held him a lifetime ago. She burned.

∞

When Charlie looked up again, the dust-devil stood outside the window, grinning and smacking her mouth.

Her lips were half gone. Stringy red tissue lined one side of her jaw. The skin had been stripped from most of her neck so that just a thin layer held in the muscles and tendons and vocal cords. Charlie could see them move when the old woman swallowed and smiled and said, thickly, "Sick."

Magdalena screamed, "No!" and Charlie grabbed her and they ran down the aisle of the luncheonette, past the astonished waitress and the round dessert display cases and the stacks of salt and pepper shakers on trays, through the swinging doors into a small kitchen full of smoke from the grill and steam from the hot water in the dishwashing sink. Charlie coughed, and his eyes stung. He could not see which way to go. He put his hand down on the counter beside him and felt wood and metal, the handle of a vegetable knife. When he picked up his hand, the knife was still in it. He stared at it for a moment like he was not sure what it was, then his mouth tightened and he slid it into his jacket pocket. Magdalena watched him without a word.

He led her out the flimsy, grease-streaked back door into an alley. At the next corner, they caught up with a bus. Charlie knew he could not afford to be picky about their destination, but it made him nervous that the bus was heading south. Downtown. He felt hounded, cornered. The knife bounced gently in his pocket as the bus swung out from the curb. Magdalena glowed beside him.

He did not see the dust-devil whirl into shape at the corner as the bus pulled away. The lipless mouth smiled, hummed, and this time it was the cold voice, the metal concrete steel diesel voice that wanted Magdalena's heart.

"I never wanted to hurt anyone," Magdalena said. She said it to Charlie but it was as if she were talking to herself. "I love this city. It's the only place I've ever belonged. I'd give anything to undo this." She squeezed his hand tight.

Storm clouds were clustered over the Loop when the bus pulled onto State Street. The pedestrian mall was deserted. Charlie and Magdalena stared as the bus rolled past boarded storefronts, waist-high piles of broken glass, twisted sewer gratings. Sand trickled from the corners of eroding skyscrapers. Grainy sour air swept in on them as the pneumatic doors opened. Charlie touched the knife in his jacket pocket like a talisman and helped Magdalena down to the street. They walked through the mall, sidestepping the holes where the sidewalk had cracked open.

The dust-devil was waiting as they rounded the corner.

She was bigger now, much bigger than they, a dozen feet tall and grey, not human; her saucer-eyes were the lamps of the subway trains as they rocketed through the tunnels in her heart, and the blinking lights along the runways at the airports, and the red and gold and green of the traffic signals; her arms and hands and legs were the steel beams of the buildings and the rails beneath the trains and the wood supports of the docks at lakeside; her breath, her voice as she roared were the scream of fire engines and the screams of the dying, the shouts of stadium crowds, the voice of everyone who had ever passed over the pavement of the city, Charlie's voice, and Magdalena's.

And the dust-devil reached for Magdalena, and Charlie tried to move, but Magdalena was already there, her hand in and out of his pocket too quick for him to catch, her hand pushing him aside, her face lifted up, her arms lifted up, the knife poised over her bared left wrist and slashing down, cut and bleed, down again, cut and bleed, over and over along the length of her arm until blood spurted and spewed from a half-dozen hacks into skin and sinew and artery. She held up her arm like a prize as her knees gave way and she went down.

And Charlie shouted, "No!" and fell forward toward her, and she moaned, "No," as she watched her skin knit up before her eyes into tight, pink scars, and, "Yes," hissed the city as it twisted toward her in a whirlwind of grey. Charlie held Magdalena's arms, tried to pull her back, but she looked so deep at him and smiled, so he knew, and his heart died then but he let her go.

She fell backward into the spitting, spiraling cloud, and was sucked in, and then was gone.

The dust-devil shrank, and slowed. For many moments it spun lightly on its point while Charlie stared and tried to make his mind work again.

An air current, like the touch of a hand, brushed his face. The dust-devil fragmented and vanished. A gardenia fell from the air and landed near Charlie's knee where he crouched on pavement that, already, was repairing itself. He touched the plump petals gently and watched the city knit itself together around him. He watched for a long time. Then he stood slowly and moved away, and let the flower lay on the sidewalk, as if it were something precious he had planted and left there to grow.

Eye of the Storm

I am a child of war. It's a poor way to start. My village was always ready to defend, or to placate, or to burn again. Eventually the fighting stopped, and left dozens of native graves and foreign babies. We war bastards banded together by instinct; most of us had the straw hair and flat faces of westerners, and we were easy marks. Native kids would find one or two of us alone and build their adrenaline with shouts of *Your father killed my father* until someone took the first step in with a raised arm or a stick. These encounters always ended in blood and cries—until the year I was fifteen, when a gang of village young played the daily round of kill-the-bastard and finally got it right: when Ad Homrun's older brother pulled her from under a pile of screaming boys and girls, and Ad's neck was broken and her right eye had burst. The others vanished like corn spirits and left us alone in a circle of trampled grass, Ad lying in Tom's arms, me trying to hold her head up at the right angle so she would breathe again. It was my first grief.

It was no wonder our kind were always vanishing in the night. "You'll go too," my mother said for the first time when I was only seven. She would often make pronouncements as she cooked. I learned her opinions on everything from marjoram ("Dry it in bundles of six sticks and keep it away from dogs") to marriage ("Some cows feel safest in the butcher's barn") while she kneaded bread or stripped slugs off fresh-picked greens.

It shocked me to hear her talk about my leaving as if it were already done. Ad was still alive in her family's cottage a quarter mile from ours, and I believed that my world was settled; not perfect, but understandable, everything fast in its place. I peered from my corner by the fire while my mother pounded corn into meal, jabbing the pestle in my direction like a finger to make her point. "You'll go," she repeated. "Off to soldier, no doubt. Born to it, that's why. No one can escape what they're born to."

"I won't," I said.

"You'll go and be glad to."

"I won't! I want to stay with you."

"Hmph," she replied, but at supper she gave me an extra corn cake with a dab of honey. Food was love as well as livelihood for her. She never punished me for being got upon her while her man screamed himself dead in the next room; but she never touched me or anyone else unless she had to. I grew up with food instead of kisses. I ate pastries and hot bread and sausage pies like a little goat, and used them as fuel to help me run faster than my tormentors.

One of the childhood games Ad and I played was to wrap up in sheepskin and swan up and down the grass between her cottage and the lane, pretending to be princes in disguise. We were both tall, after all, and looked noble in our woolly cloaks. What more did one need? To be the first child of a king, Tom Homrun said, and our king already had one. There could only be one prince, only one heir. The rest were just nobles, and there were more of them than anyone bothered to count. *What's the good of being a royal if you're as common as ticks on a dog?* my mother would say, with a cackle for her own wit. But I had heard too many stories about the prince. My aunt's third husband went to court for a meeting of royal regional accountants and told us in his letters that the prince was fair and strong and already had the air of a leader. *And puts me in mind of your Mars*, he wrote my mother; *something about the eyes.* My mother paused after she'd read that part aloud, and looked at me with a still face. It thrilled me to be likened to the prince, and Ad was rigid with envy until Tom carved her a special stick to use as a sceptre in our games, with a promise that he would never make me one no matter how hard I pleaded. I could not care about her stick, about her silence and hurt feelings, even though she was my only friend. My head was full of daydreams of walking through the streets of Lemon City, of being seen by the prince's retainers and taken up into the citadel, marveled over, embraced, offered…what? My imagination failed me there, so I would start from the beginning and see it all again. I began giving the pigs orders, and delivering speeches of state to the group of alder trees near Nor Tellit's farm.

They were different speeches after Ad died. At first they were simply incoherent weepings delivered from a throat so thick with snot that I barely recognized my own voice. It sounded adult and terrible, and filled me with a furious energy I didn't know how to use; until one afternoon when I ran dry of tears and instead picked up a fist-sized stone. I beat the alders until the rock was speckled with my blood. I washed my swollen hand in the village well and hoped my rage would poison them all. Then I found Tom Homrun and asked him to teach me how to fight.

From the first I was like a pig at a slop pile, gulping down whatever he put in front of me, always rooting single-mindedly for more. He taught me to use my hands and elbows and knees, to judge distance, and to watch someone's body rather than their eyes. It was hard at first to trust him and his teaching: I'd always thought of him as a native, as a danger, in spite of his fondness for his yellow-haired bastard sister. And it hadn't occurred to me that he would have to touch me. Apart from Ad, I'd only touched my mother by accident, and the village kids in desperate defense: but this was new and electric. The first feel of his muscle against mine was so shocking that the hair on my arms and legs stood up. I was desperately uneasy to think that I might be moved by Tom after what I'd begun to feel for his sister, as if it were some kind of betrayal of Ad. But I was fascinated by the strength and power of his body, the way it turned when he wished, held its balance, reached out and so easily made me vulnerable.

I was just sixteen when we began, and the sky was always grey with the start or end of snow. I learned to move when I was too cold, too sore, too tired. I learned to keep going. All the things I wanted—Ad, my mother, a life of endless hard blue days in the fields, and just one true friend with dark hair and a father still alive—all those precious things became buried under a crust of long outlander muscles. I began to imagine myself an arrow laid against the string, ready to fly. I looked at the village kids with my arrow's eyes, and they stayed out of my way.

By summer I knew enough not to knock myself silly. I was tired of the same exercises and hungry now for more than just revenge: I wanted to be a warrior. "Show me how to use a sword," I begged Tom constantly, sometimes parrying an invisible adversary with a long stick.

"No," he said for the hundredth time.

"Why not?"

"There's no point until you get your full growth. You're tall as me now, but you might make another inch or two before you're done."

"You didn't make me wait to learn how to fight."

"Swords are different. They change your balance. You've got to make the sword part of yourself, it's not enough just to pick it up and wave it around. It's true that you've learned well," he added. "But you haven't learned everything."

"Then teach me everything."

"Leave it alone, Mars."

I had no idea I was going to do it: I had never given him anything but the obedience due a teacher. But I was so frustrated with behaving. "You teach me, damn you," I said, and swung the stick as hard as I could at his ribs.

He softened against the blow and absorbed it. The stick was dry and thin, but still it must have hurt. It sounded loud, perhaps because we were both so silent.

I stammered, "Tom, truly, I was wrong to do it, I just…"

"You're stupid, Mars." His voice was very quiet. "You're not the strongest, you never will be, and no sword will change that. I'm heavier and faster than you, and there's thousands more like me out there." He waved at the world beyond the fields, and when I turned my head, he reached out and twisted the branch away as easily as taking a stick from a puppy. "All you have are your wits and your body, if you can ever learn how to use them."

What had we been doing, all these months? "I can use my body."

A bruise I'd given him at the corner of his mouth stretched into a purple line. Then his smile changed into the stiff look that people wear when they are forcing themselves to a thing they'd rather not do; like the day he'd had to butcher Ad's favorite nanny goat while she cried into my shoulder. I did not like him looking at me as if I were that goat.

"You want to learn everything." He nodded. "Well, then you shall." And he came for me.

I managed to keep him off me for more than a minute, a long stretch of seconds that burned the strength from the muscles in my arms and legs. But he was right; he was too strong, too fast. First he got me down and then he beat me, his face set, his hands like stones against my ribs and my face. His last blow was to my nose, and when he finally stood up, he was spattered with me.

"This is everything, Mars. This is what I have to teach you. Become the weapon. Do it, and no one will touch you in a fight. Otherwise it's only a matter of time before someone sends you to the next world in pieces."

I was trying to spit instead of swallow; it made it harder to breathe, and every cough jarred my broken nose.

"I regret this," he said remotely. "But every time we meet from now on will be like this until you win or you quit. If you quit, I'll teach you nothing ever again. That's the lesson. I don't think you can do it, you know. I don't think you're ready. I wish you hadn't pushed so hard." He spoke as if he were talking to a stranger on the road.

He left me at the field's edge, under a creamy blue sky and the alders that were scarred with months of practice; all those pointless hours. After a long time I dragged myself up and limped home, turning my head away as I passed the Homrun cottage so that I would not have to see whether Tom was watching. I let my mother bind my ribs, avoiding her questions and the silence that followed. Then I wrapped myself up in wool blankets and shivered all night, bruised and betrayed, frightened, and hopelessly alone.

He beat me badly half a dozen times in the next year. Between our fights, I practiced and worked and invented a thousand different ways to keep distance between us, to protect my body from his. None of it made a speck of difference.

The day came when I knew I could never win. There was no grand omen, no unmistakable sign. I was milking our goat, and I suddenly understood that Tom was right. Someone would always be faster or stronger, and until I learned my place I would always be hurt and lonely. It was time to make peace and stop dreaming of Lemon City. I should be planning a fall garden, and tending Ad's grave. So there, it was decided; and I went on pulling methodically at the little goat's dry teats until she bleated impatiently and kicked at me to let her go. Then I sat on the milking stump and stared around me at the cottage, the tall birch that shaded it, the yard with the goat and the chickens, the half-tumbled stone wall that bounded our piece of the world. If someone had come by and said, "What are you looking at, Mars?", I would have said *Nothing. Nothing.*

Massive storm clouds began moving up over my shoulder from the west. The shadow of the birch across the south wall faded, and the chickens scuttled into their coop and tucked themselves up in a rattling of feathers. The wind turned fierce and cold; and then the rain hammered down. I hunched on the stump until it occurred to me that I was freezing, that I should see that the stock were safe and then get inside; and when I tried to stand the wind knocked me over like a badly pitched fence post. I pulled myself up. Again the wind shoved me down. And again. This time I landed on one of my half-dozen unhealed bruises. It hurt; and it made me so angry that I forgot about my numb hands and my despair. I stood again. There was a loud *snap* behind me. It took a long second to turn against the wind: by that time, the branch that the storm had torn from the birch tree was already slicing toward me like a thrown spear.

I took a moment to understand what was happening, to imagine the wood knifing through me, to see my grave next to Ad's. Then the branch reached me, and I slid forward and to the right as if to welcome it; and as we touched I whirled off and away, staggered but kept my balance, and watched the branch splinter against the shed. The goat squealed from behind the wall; and I laughed from my still, safe place at the center of the storm.

⤙

I had an idea now, and the only way to test it was by getting beaten again, and so I did: but not as badly.

When he'd finally let me up, Tom said, as always, "Do you give in?"

"No."

He was supposed to turn and walk away. Instead, he kept hold of my tunic with his left hand and wiped his bleeding mouth with his right. He took his time. Then he said, "What was that first move?"

I shrugged.

"Who taught you that?"

I shrugged again, as much as I was able with one shoulder sprained.

"I expect I'll be ready for it, next time." He opened his hand and dropped me on my back in the dirt, and set off down the road toward the village. He favored his right leg just slightly: it was the first sign of pain he had ever shown. But that wasn't what made me feel so good, what made the blood jizzle under my skin: it was the way I'd felt fighting him. I treated him just like the flying birch limb—allowed him close, so close that we became a single storm; and for a moment I was our center and I spun him as easily as if I were a wind and he a bent branch.

The next time went better for me, and the time after that. It became a great dance, a wild game, to see how close I could get to him, how little I could twist away and remain out of reach, just beyond his balance point. He was heavier than me, differently muscled: it taught me to go beyond strength and look instead for the instant of instability, the moment when I could make him overreach himself. It was exhilarating to enter into his dangerous space and turn his weapons against him; it was delicious to be most safe when I was closest to my enemy. I didn't notice my hurts anymore, except when parts of me stopped working. Then I would retreat to my corner by the cottage fire, sipping comfrey tea and reliving each moment, sucking whatever learning I could from the memory of each blow. My body and his became the whole of my world.

And the world was changing. I got those last two inches of growth and my body flung itself frantically into adulthood. I suppose it must have been happening all along underneath the sweat and the bruises and the grinding misery. But now that I was noticing it, it seemed to have come upon me all at once, and it was a different feeling from the days when Ad's smile could make me feel impossibly clever. This was the lust I'd seen at the dark edges of the village common after the harvest celebration, the thing of skin and wordless noise. No one had told me it would feel like turning into an arrow from the inside out and wanting nothing more than something to sink myself into. Sometimes it was so strong that I would have thrown myself on the next person I met, if only there had been anyone who wouldn't have thrown me right back. But there was no one. I could only burn and rage and stuff it all back into the whirlwind inside me: make myself a storm.

And so one day I finally won, and it was Tom who lay on one elbow, spitting blood. When the inside of his mouth had clotted, he said, "Well." Then we were both silent for a while.

"Well," he said later.

And: "You'll be fine now. You're a match for anyone, the way you fight. It's okay to let you go now. You'll be safe."

And then he began to cry. When I bent over him to see if he was hurt more badly than I thought, he gripped my arm and kissed me. He did not stop me when I pulled

away, and he did not try to hide his tears. I didn't understand then the kind of love that kills itself to make the be-
loved safe: I only knew my world had shaken itself apart
and come back together in a way that did not include me
anymore.

I told my mother that night that I would leave in a
week. She did not speak, and all I could say over and over
was "I have to go," as if it were an apology or a plea. Later
as I sat miserably in front of the fire, she touched the back
of my head so softly that I wasn't sure if I was meant to
feel it. Her fingers on my hair told me that she grieved,
and that her fear for me was like sour milk on the back of
her tongue; and that in spite of it all she forgave me for
becoming myself, for growing up into someone who could
suddenly remind her of how she got me. I had traded
scars and bruises with the village kids for years, but never
before had I hurt someone I loved just by being myself;
and in one day I had done it to the only two people left to
me. And so I felt my world hitch and shake like a wet dog,
and my choices fell over me like drops of dirty water: none
of them clean.

I set off early, just past dawn. Over breakfast, my
mother said, "Here's a thing for you," and handed me a
long bundle. When I unwrapped it, the lamplight flick-
ered across the blade inside and my mother's sad and
knowing eyes.

"Don't look at me," she said. "That Tom Homrun
brought it around three days past and said I wasn't to give
it to you until you were leaving."

There was no scabbard. I made a secure place for the sword in my belt, across my left hip.

"Feel like a proper soldier now, I expect," my mother said quietly.

"I just feel all off balance," I told her, and she smiled a little.

"You'll be all right, then." She nodded, then sighed, stood up, fussed with my slingbag. "I've put up some traveling food for you. And a flask of water as well, you never know when the next spring might be dry."

I tried to smile.

"Which way are you heading?"

"East. In-country."

She nodded again. "I thought you might head west."

"Mum!" I was shocked. "Those are our enemies."

"You've had more enemies here than ever came out of the west, child," she said. "I just wondered."

I took a breath. "I would never do anything to hurt you, Mum. You've been nothing but good to me." Another breath. "Tell Tom…give him my thanks." Opening the door, the damp, grey air in my face. "I love you, Mum." Kissing her dry cheek. "I love you." Three steps out now, her standing in the door, half in shadow, one hand to her face. "Goodbye, Mum." Four more steps, walking backwards now, still looking at her. "Goodbye." Turning away; walking away; leaving. Her voice catching up with me, "I've loved you, Mars. Godspeed." The bend in the road.

I was alone on the road for a week. Every day brought me something new: a stand of unfamiliar trees, a stream of green water, a red-hooded bird that swooped from tree to tree above me for a hundred paces before it flashed away into the woods. I walked steadily. I didn't think about home or the future. I became more thin. I played with the sword. It wasn't balanced well for me, but I thought a good smith could remedy that, and meanwhile I learned not to overreach myself with the new weight at the end of my arm. Carrying it on my hip gave me a persistent pain in my lower back, until I found a rolling walk that brought the sword forward without swinging it into my leg at each step. Ad would have called it swagger, but she would have liked it. There was one moment, in a yellow afternoon just as the road lifted itself along the rim of a valley, when I could hear her laugh as if she were only a step behind me, and I missed her as fiercely as in the first month after her death. And I kept going.

On the eighth day I met people.

I heard them before I saw them; two speaking, maybe more silent in their group. I stopped short and found myself sweating, as if their sound was warm water bubbling through the top layer of my skin. I hadn't thought at all about what to do with other people. I had met less than a dozen strangers in my life.

"I think there's something in the wood," one of the voices said brightly.

"A wolf?" A hint of laughter.

"A bear."

"A giant."

"A creature with the body of an eagle and a pig's head and teeth as big as your hands."

I was beginning to feel ridiculous; it made me move again. I came out of the trees into an open place where my road met another running north and south. Just beyond the crossroads, three people sat with their backs against a low stone wall that bounded a meadow. I slowed my step. I had no idea how one behaved, and I'm sure it showed. The woman who called to me had the same glittery amusement in her voice that I'd heard as she'd described all the fabulous monsters I might be.

"Why, it's not a bear. Ho, traveler." She nodded. I felt awkward, and I wondered if my voice would work properly after so long in its own company; so I only returned her nod, hitched up my belt, and kept walking. As soon as it was clear that I meant to pass them by, she scrambled to her feet, scattering breadcrumbs and a piece of cheese out of her lap into the grass. "Luck, don't," the man said, and grabbed but missed her. She darted toward me. I turned to face her, my hands out, waiting.

"Ah ha," she said, and stopped out of my reach. "Perhaps a bear cub after all. I don't mean to detain you against your will, traveler. We have Shortline cheese to share, and we'd welcome news of the world beyond this road."

She was relaxed, smiling, but she watched my body rather than my face, and her knees were slightly bent, ready to move her in whatever direction she needed to go. She looked strong and capable, but I could see a weakness in her stance, a slight cant to her hips. *I could probably take her*, I thought.

I put my hands down. "The place I've come from is so small, you'd miss it if you looked down to scratch. But I can trade flatcakes for a wedge of cheese and your news."

"Fair enough," she said.

She was Lucky, and the man was Ro. The other, silent woman was Braxis. We ate cheese and my mother's cake in the afternoon sun, and they told me about the North, and I gave them what I knew about the West. I was nervous, but gradually their laughter, their worldliness, won me over. They never asked a question that was too personal, and they gave exactly as much information about themselves as I did, so I never felt at a disadvantage.

"What is it you want from me?" I asked finally. I don't know exactly what made me say it. Maybe it was the combination of the warm gold sun and the warm gold cheese, the bread and the cider from Braxis' wine-skin. Maybe it was hearing about the great cities to the north, Shirkasar and Low Grayling, and the massive port of Hunemoth, the way they made me see the marketplaces and the moonlight on the marbled plazas of the noble houses. Maybe it was the looks the three of them traded when I answered their questions.

Braxis raised an eyebrow in my direction. It was Ro who answered.

"Okay, so you know when something's going on under your nose. That's good. Can you fight?"

I tensed. "I've told you how I grew up. I can fight."

"We're going to Lemon City, to the auditions. We need a fourth."

"What auditions?"

"Hoo hoo," Lucky said with a grin.

"Three times a year they hold an audition for the city guard," Ro said. "They only accept quads, they think it's the most stable configuration for training and fighting."

"So," I said. I thought of Tom under the alders, of Lemon City as I'd imagined it with Ad.

"So you probably noticed there are only three of us."

"You came all this way from Grayling without a fourth?"

"No, of course not," Ro said patiently. "He left us two days ago. He found true love in some stupid little town with probably only one bloodline, but he didn't care. He's a romantic, much good may it do him in the ass end of nowhere."

"And you'd take me just like that, not knowing me at all."

"What do we need to know?" Lucky said. "You breathe, you can stand up without falling over. You're on the road to Lemon City, aren't you? Do you want a job or not?"

"You mean for money?" She shook her head as if she couldn't credit my being so dumb. But I'd expected to have to find honest work, meaning something dirty and bone-tiring, before I could start looking for someone to train with. The idea of getting tired, dirty, and paid to train was so exciting I could hardly believe it was real.

Ro said, "We'll offer you a trial on the road. Travel with us to Lemon City, and we'll see if we want to take it any farther."

"Not without a fight," Braxis said. We all looked at her; Ro and Lucky seemed as surprised that she'd spoken as they did at what she'd said.

"I don't take anyone on without knowing if they can hold their own," she said reasonably. "Not even on trial. That's the whole point of a quad, isn't it? Four walls, stable house. We need strong walls."

"They train you, Brax," Ro responded. "All we have to do is get past the gate."

"No," I said slowly. "She's right. And so are you: I do want to go to Lemon City, but it's got to be properly done." They looked at me with a variety of expressions: Braxis impassive, Ro with his head tilted and a wrinkle in his forehead, Lucky grinning with her arms akimbo.

"I can't explain it. But I need this to be something I can be proud of. It needs to be earned."

"Gods, another romantic," Ro muttered.

We climbed over the wall into the field, and laid aside our swords. Lemon City was just behind that cloud, and I was a hot wind. It was such an amazing feeling that I almost forgot I'd never really fought anyone except Tom, that I didn't yet know if I could. Then Braxis' strong arms reached for me.

When we were done, and Brax had finished coughing up grass, she said, "Fine. On the way there, you can teach us how to do that."

<hr>

We began to learn each other: Braxis woke up surly; Lucky sang walking songs out of tune, and she knew a hundred of them; Ro was good at resolving differences between others and peevish when he didn't get his own way. I wasn't sure what they were discovering about me. I'd never lived with anyone except my mother: it was one more thing I didn't know how to do. I watched everything and tried not to offend anyone.

We got into the routine of making camp early in the afternoon, to keep the last hours of light for practicing swords and stormfighting. It didn't take them long to work out that I barely knew one end of my sword from the other. I was ashamed, and halfway expected them to kick me back up the road. They surprised me. "I've never seen anyone fight like you do," Ro said matter-of-factly. "If we can trade learning between us, it makes us all stronger." Then he set about showing me the basics.

Two weeks later it was Lucky who came toward me with her sword. I looked at Ro. He smiled. "I've given you enough so that you can at least keep up with what she's got to show you. She's the best of us."

I expected the thrust-and-parry exercises that I'd worked on with Ro, but Lucky came to stand to one side of me, just out of blade range. She extended her sword. "Follow me," was all she said, and then she was off in a step, turn, strike, block that moved straight into a new combination. She was fast. I stayed with her as best I could, and actually matched her about one move in seven.

"Not horrible," she said. "Let's try it again." We worked it over and over until finally she reached out and pried the sword out of my grip. "Those will hurt tomorrow," she said of the blisters on my palms. "You should have told me." But I was determined to hold my own with these people, so I only shrugged. My hands felt raw for days after; but I was stubborn. And it helped that I could teach as well as learn. It did not matter so much that I was the youngling, the inexperienced one, when their bodies worked to imitate mine, when their muscles fluttered and strained to please me.

And I had a new secret: I was beginning to understand the price for all those months that I'd wrestled my body's feelings back into my fighting. I could scrub Lucky's back after a cold creek bath, see Brax's nipples crinkle when she shrugged off her shirt at night, lie with my head pillowed on Ro's thigh—and never feel a thing except a growing sense of wonder at what complex and contradictory people I had found on my road. But when we met in practice, everything changed. The slide of Brax's leather-covered breast against my arm during a takedown put a point of heat at the tip of every nerve from my shoulder to my groin. Ro's weight on me when he tested the possibilities of a technique was voluptuous in a way I'd never imagined in my awkward days with Ad. Lucky's rain-wet body twisting underneath me excited me so much it was almost beyond bearing: but I learned to bear it, to stuff the pleasure back inside myself so that it wound through me endlessly, like a cloud boiling with the weight of unreleased rain. In my days with Tom I had learned to fight through cold and pain and misery: now I learned to persist through pleasure so keen that sometimes it left me seared and breathless and not sure how to make my arms and legs keep working. I told no one; but I woke in the morning anticipating those hours, and slept at night with their taste in my throat. I was always ready to practice.

"I sweat like a bull," Brax said ruefully one day when we were all rubbing ourselves down afterwards. "But you always smell so good." I smiled and pulled my tunic on quickly to hide the shudders that still trembled through me.

It was a few days later that Ro approached me after supper, squatting down beside me near the fire. We smiled at each other and spent a quiet time stripping the bark off sticks and feeding it to the flames. Eventually, he said, "Share my blanket tonight?"

I'd seen from the first night how it was between them, bedding two at a time but in a relationship of three. I had already guessed at their idea of what a quad should be. I wondered how sophisticated people handled this sort of thing.

"No, but thank you," I said finally. "It's not you, Ro, you're a fine person, and I'm pleased to be part of your quad. It's just—"

"No need to explain," he said, which only made me feel more awkward. But the next day he treated me not much differently. By the afternoon I had recovered my equilibrium, and I'd noticed their quiet conversations, so I was only a little surprised to find Lucky at my elbow after practice.

"Let's take a walk," she said cheerfully. "Fetch water, or something."

"Fine," I said, and went to gather everyone's waterskins. "No need to rush," Braxis said. Ro nodded agreeably.

"Fine," I said again, and off we went.

We found a stream and loaded up with water, and then sat on the bank. I laid back with my head on my arms while Lucky fiddled with flower stems. Then she leaned over me and kissed me. Her mouth was dry and sweet. But nothing moved in me. I sat up and set her back from me as gently as I could. She didn't look angry, only amused. "Would Braxis have been a better choice for water duty today?"

"No, it's not that."

"Don't you know what you like, then?"

"You know what?" I said, "Let's go back to the others so I only have to have this conversation once."

We all sat around, and they chewed on hand-sized chunks of bread while I talked.

"Anyone would be proud to have you as lovers, all of you." It was nice to see the way they glowed for each other then, with nothing more than smiles or a quick touch before turning their attention back to me. "It's not about you."

I stopped, long enough that Braxis raised an eyebrow. It was hard to say the next thing. "If you need that from your fourth, then I'll help you find someone else when we get to Lemon City, and no hard feelings."

We were all quiet for a while. Finally Braxis wiped the crumbs off her hands. "Oh, well," she said. "Of course we don't want another fourth, Mars, we'd rather have you even if we can't have you, if you take my meaning." Lucky hooted, and I went red in the face, which just made Lucky worse.

"No, truly," Braxis went on when Ro had finally put a hammerlock on Lucky. "We like you. We're start-ing to fight well together. We learn from each other. We trust ourselves. We can be a good quad. The other," she shrugged, and Lucky made a rude gesture, "well, it's nice, but it isn't everything, is it?"

It stayed with me, that remark, while I did my share of the night chores, and later as I lay on my back in the dark, listening to Ro's snores and the small, eager sounds that Braxis and Lucky made together under a restless sky of black scudding clouds. It was strange to think about sex with them so intent on it just a knife-throw away. *It's nice but it's not everything*, Brax had said: but for those moments it sounded like it was everything for the two of them.

I hoped they stayed willing to take me as I was. I didn't know if I could explain that what they did wrapped in their blankets was like being offered the lees of fine wine. I could tell they thought I was still grieving for Ad, or Tom: let them believe that, if it would obscure the truth of what I had become and what stirred me now. *Keep your mouth shut, Mars*, I told myself, and twisted onto my side away from them. *They'll never understand and you'd never be able to explain. They'll think you're insane or perverted or worse, and they'll send you packing back to your no-name village before you can say "Oh go ahead and fuck me if that's what it takes to let me stay with you."*

I never was much good at cheering myself up: but in spite of it all I finally fell asleep, and I woke to a hug from Braxis and pine tea from Ro, to a sleepy pat on the shoulder from Lucky, and for the first time in oh-so-long I felt the hope of belonging.

⟵

It took weeks to get to Lemon City, mostly because we were in no hurry. There was always so much to do each day, so much exploring and talking and the hands-on work of turning ourselves into a fighting partnership. And other kinds of work, as well. In spite of what they'd said, the three of them made a concerted effort to seduce me, and I didn't know how to reassure them that they already had, that they had turned me into a banked coal with a constant fire in my belly. "Damn your cold heart, Mars," Lucky spat at me one day, "I hope someday someone you really want turns you down flat, and then see how you like it!"

"Luck, it's not like that!" I called out after her as she stalked off down a side trail into the woods.

"Leave her," Ro advised. "She'll accept it. We all will." He and Brax exchanged a wry look, and I felt terrible. I must be cold, I thought, cold and selfish. It was such a small thing to ask, to make people I loved happy. But it wasn't just my body they wanted, it was me, and they would never reach me that way, and then we would all still be unsatisfied. And I was not willing to explain. So it was my fault, my flaw. My failure.

I was packing my bedroll when Lucky came back. "Oh, stop," she said impatiently. "You know what I'm like, Mars, don't take it so personally. Just stay away from me tonight and I'll be fine in the morning." And she was; and the next afternoon, when she took hold of me so unknowingly, I gave her myself. I gave to all of them, a dozen times each day.

"The hardest part about all this," Brax said one evening as we all stretched out near our fire, "is overcoming all the sword training."

"Whaddya mean?" Ro mumbled around a mouthful of cheese.

"Well, the sword makes your arm longer and gives it a killing edge, so that you still strike or punch, sort of, but it's with the blade. But the stormfighting, well, like Mars is always saying, the whole point is to become the center of the fight and bring your enemy in to you. So with the sword we keep people out far enough to slice them up, and with the storm art we bring them in close enough to kiss. It does my head in sometimes trying to figure out where I'm supposed to be when."

"You think it's hard for you?" I replied. "You're not the one with half a dozen cuts on every arm and leg trying to learn it the other way around. I always let Lucky get too close."

"So maybe there's a way to do both." Lucky reached out to swipe a piece of cheese from Ro's lap.

"What do you mean?" Ro asked again.

"Pig. Give me some of that. I mean that maybe there's a way to combine the moves. All the sword dances I do are based on wheels, being able to turn and move in any direction with your body and the sword like spokes on a wheel. It's not that different from being at the center of a wind, or whatever."

"Gods around us," I said. She'd put a picture in my mind so clear that for a moment I wasn't sure which was more real, the Lucky who smiled quizzically at me from across the fire, or the one who suddenly rolled over her own sword and came up slashing at her opponent's knee. "She's right. You could do both. Think about it! Just think about it!" They were all bright-eyed now, caught in the spiral of my excitement that drew them in as surely as one of the armlocks we'd worked on that afternoon. "Imagine being able to fight long or short, with an edge or a tip or just your bare hand. They'd never know what to expect, they couldn't predict what you'd do next!"

"Okay, maybe," Lucky said. "It might work with that whole series that's based off the step in and behind, but what about the face-to-face? A sword's always a handicap when you're in that close."

"That's because everyone always goes weapon to weapon." Lucky looked blank. "If you have a sword, what's the other person going to do? Get a bigger sword if they can. Try to beat your sword. But we don't need that. Our weapon is the way we fight. Go in and take their sword away. Go in and do things with a sword that no one thinks possible. In my head I just saw you roll with your own blade and come up edge-ready. Maybe staying low would give us more options for being in close."

"Come here," Lucky said, and scrambled up, and we worked it out again and again until the fire was almost dead and we trod on Brax in the dark. "Stop this idiocy and go to sleep!" she growled; but the next day we were all ready to reinvent sword fighting, and we ate our dinner that night bloody and bruised and grinning like children.

⤙

We came into Lemon City on a cold wind, just ahead of a hard autumn rain that dropped from a fast front of muddy clouds. We crowded under cover of a blacksmith's shed inside the city gates with a dozen other travelers, three gate guards, and two bad-tempered horses, while manure and straw and someone's basket washed away down the waterlogged street. Everything was grey and stinking. I couldn't help laughing, remembering my fantasies about the golden streets full of important people in silk with me in the center, being whisked toward greatness.

When the rain had passed we walked in towards the heart of the city. My boots leaked, and my feet got wet, and Ro stepped in goat shit and swore.

"So far, I feel right at home," I told Lucky, who cackled wildly and reminded me for one sharp moment of my mother, bent over in laughter with her hands twisted in her apron and flour dust rising all around her.

We found an inn that they'd heard of, and got the second-to-last room left. We were lucky; the last room was no better than a sty, and went an hour later for the same rate as ours. The city was packed tighter than a farm sausage, our landlord told us with a satisfied smile. He took some of Ro's money for a pitcher of cider and settled one hip against the common room table to tell us where to find the guard house for the coming auditions. The next were in two days' time. "And lots of competition for this one, of course," he said cheerfully, with a glance around the crowded room that made him scurry to another table with his tray of cider.

"What's that mean, of course?" Lucky wondered when he'd gone away.

I shrugged. Brax drank the last of her cider. "I hate it when they say of course," she muttered, and belched.

The next day was sunny, and we went out exploring. I left my sword for the day with the blacksmith near the city gate, who promised to lengthen the grip. From there we wandered to the market, and they laughed at my wide-eyed amazement. And everywhere we saw foursomes, young or seasoned, trying not to show their stress by keeping their faces impassive, so of course you could spot them a mile off. We followed some of them to the guards training camp, and waited in line to give our names to someone whose only job that day seemed to be telling stiff-faced hopefuls where and when to turn up for the next morning's trials. Then we found a place to perch where Lucky and Brax could size everyone up until they found something to feel superior about: a weak eye, too much weight on one foot, someone's hands looped under their belt so they couldn't reach their weapon easily. Eventually the strain got to be too much, and we went back to the inn for an afternoon meal and practice on a small patch of ground near the stable. Working up a sweat seemed to calm them down; and touching them erased everything else for me.

That night, I laid an extra coin on the table when the landlord brought our platter of chicken and pitcher of beer, and said, "Tell us what's so special about these auditions."

He looked genuinely surprised. "Anybody could tell you that," he said, but he put the coin in his sleeve pocket.

"The prince has turned out half the palace guard again, and Captain Gerlain's scrambling for replacements. Those who do well are sure to end up with palace duty, although why any of you'd want it is beyond me."

"Why's that?"

"Our prince is mad, that's why, and the king's too far gone up his own backside to notice."

Lucky put a hand to her knife. "You mind yourself, man," she said calmly, and Brax and I tried not to grin at each other. Lucky could be startlingly conservative.

"Oh, and no offense intended to the king," he said easily. "But well done, the king needs loyal soldiers around him. Particularly now he's old and sick, and too well medicated, at least that's what they say. You just get yourself hired on up there and keep an eye on him for us." He poured Lucky another drink. I admired the skill with which he'd turned the conflict aside.

None of us could eat, thinking about the next day, and the beer tasted off. We sat at the table, not talking much. Eventually we moved out to the snug, where the landlord had a fire going. It was warmer there than the common room, but no more relaxing. I turned the coming day over and over in my head as if it were a puzzle I couldn't put down until I'd solved it. Lucky and Ro sat close together: their calves touched, then their thighs, then Ro's hand found its way onto Lucky's arm and she sighed, leaned into him, looking suddenly small and soft. When I looked away, Brax was there, next to me.

She cupped her hard hand around my jaw and cheek and left ear. "Don't turn me away, Mars," she said quietly. "It's no night to be alone."

"You're right," I replied. "But let's try something a little different." I felt wild and daring, even though I knew she wouldn't understand. I took her by the hand and led her out to our practice area by the stable. They kept a lantern out there for late arrivals; it gave us just enough light to see motion, but the fine work would have to be done by instinct: by feel.

"You want to practice?" she said.

My heart was thudding under my ribs. This was the closest I had ever come to telling anyone what it was like with me. It was so tempting to say *Take me down, Brax, challenge me, control me, equal me, best me, love me.* But I only smiled and stepped into the small circle of light. "Put your hands on me," I whispered, soft enough so that she would not hear, and centered myself.

***

They were fair auditions, and hard, and we were brilliant. I could tell they had never seen anything like us. The method was to put two quads into the arena with wooden swords. I learned later that they looked for how we fought, but that was only part of it. "The fighting is the easiest thing to teach," Captain Gerlain told me once. "What I look for is basic coordination, understanding of the body and how it works. And how the quad works together."

It was an incredible day, a blur of things swirled together: crisp air that smelled of fried bread from the camp kitchen and the sweat of a hundred nervous humans; the sounds of leather on skin and huffing breath interleaved with the faint music of temple singers practicing three streets away; and the touch of a hundred different hands, the textures of their skin, the energies that ran between us as we laid hold of one another.

After he saw our stormfighting, Gerlain started putting other quads against us, so that we fought more than anyone else. Most of the fighters didn't know what to make of us, and I began to see that Gerlain was using us as a touchstone to test the others. Those who tried to learn from us, who adapted as best they could, had the good news with us when Gerlain's sergeant read out the names at the end of the day; and Gerlain himself stopped Lucky and said, curtly, "You and your quad'll be teaching the rest an hour a day, after regular training, starting tomorrow afternoon. Work out your program with Sergeant Manto. And don't get above yourselves. Manto will be watching, and so will I."

"Hoo hoo!" said Lucky. "Let's get drunk!" But I was already intoxicated by the day, dizzy with the feel of so many strangers' skin against mine. And I was a guard. I whispered it to Ad as we walked back to the inn through the streets that now seemed familiar and welcoming. *I made it*, I told her. *Lemon City*. I thought of Tom, and my mother: *I'm safe, I found a place for myself.* I saw Ad with her sheepskin and her special stick; I felt Tom's tears on my skin, and my mother's hand on my hair. Then Ro was standing in the door to the inn, looking for me, waiting: and I went in.

It was the stormfighting that kept us out of a job for such a long time. Gerlain and Manto saw it as a tactical advantage and a way to teach warriors not to rely on their swords. Tom would have approved. But many of our fellow soldiers did not. Our frank admission that it was still raw, as dangerous to the fighter as to the target, and our matter-of-fact approach to teaching, were the only things that kept us from being permanent outsiders in the guard. Even so, we made fewer friends than we might have.

"Can't let you go yet," Manto would shrug each month, when new postings were announced. "Need you to teach the newbs."

"Let someone else teach," Ro was arguing again.

"Who? There's no one here who knows it the way you do."

"That's because you keep posting them on as soon as they've halfway learned anything."

"Shucks," Manto grinned, showing her teeth. "You noticed."

"Manto, try to see this from our point of view..."

"Oh gods," I whispered to Lucky, "There he goes, being reasonable again. Do something."

"Right," she whispered back, and then stepped between Ro and Manto, pointing a finger at Ro when he tried to protest. She said pleasantly, "We came here to be guards, not baby-minders. You want us to teach, fine, we'll teach other guards. Until then, I think we'll just go get a beer." She turned and started for the gate, hooking a thumb into Ro's belt to pull him along. Brax sighed and reached for her gear. I gave Manto a cheerful smile and a goodbye salute.

"All right, children," Manto said, pitching her voice to halt Lucky and Ro. "Report to Andavista tomorrow at the palace. Take all your toys, you'll draw quarters up there."

Even Lucky was momentarily speechless.

Manto grinned again. "The orders have been in for a couple of weeks. I just wanted to see how much more time I could get out of you." She slapped me on the arm so hard I almost fell over. "Welcome to the army."

"Where the hell have you people been?" Sergeant Andavista snarled at us the next morning. "Been waiting for you for two weeks." There seemed to be no good answer to that, so we didn't even try. "Your rooms are at the end of the southwest gallery. Unpack and report back here to me in ten minutes. Move!"

The rooms had individual beds, for which I was grateful. The double-wide bunks at the training camp had made us all more tense with one another as time went on, and I was tired of sleeping on the floor—particularly after a good day's work, when my body felt hollowed out by the thousand moments of desire roused and sated and born again, every time we grappled, when I only wanted to sleep close to one of my unknowing lovers and drink in the smell of our sweat on their skin.

Andavista handed us off to the watch commander, who gave us new gear with the palace insignia and a brain-numbing recital of guard schedules. Then she found a man just coming off watch and drafted him to show us around. The soldier looked bone-tired, but he nodded agreeably enough and tried to hide his yawns as he led us up and down seemingly endless hallways. He pointed out the usual watch stations: main gate, trade entrances, public rooms, armory, the three floors where the bureaucrats lived and worked, and the fourteen floors of nobles' chambers, which he waved at dismissively. I remembered my mother saying *ticks on a dog*.

He brought us to a massive set of wooden doors strapped with iron. "Royal suite," he said economically. "Last stop on the tour. Can you find your own way back?"

We did, although it took the better part of an hour and made us all grumpy. "Not bad," the watch commander commented when we returned. "Last week's set had to be fetched out."

And so we settled. It wasn't much different from living in my village, except that I belonged. We learned soldiery and taught stormfighting and found time to practice by ourselves, to reinforce old ideas, to invent new ones. It was an easy routine to settle to, but I'd had my lessons too well from Tom to ever relax completely, and the rest of the quad had learned to trust my edge. And it helped in a turned-around way that news of us had spread up from the training ground, and there were soldiers we'd never met who resented us for being different and were contemptuous of what they'd heard about stormfighting. Being the occasional target of pointed remarks or pointed elbows was new for Brax and Lucky and Ro; it kept them aware in a way that all my warnings never could. So on the day we found swords at our throats, we were ready.

They came for the king and prince during the midnight watch when we were stationed outside the royal wing. Ro thought he might have seen the king once, at the far end of the audience room, but these doors were the closest we had ever been to the people we were sworn to protect. And it was our first posting to this most private area of the palace. Perhaps that's why they chose our watch to try it. Or perhaps because they had dismissed the purposely slow practice drills of storm art as nothing more than fancy-fighting; it was a common enough belief among our detractors.

The first sign we had that anything was amiss was when two of the daywatch quads came up the hall. Brax stepped forward; it was her night to be in charge. "We're relieving you," their leader said. "Andavista wants you down at the gates."

"What's up?" Brax asked neutrally, but I could see the way her shoulders tensed.

The other shrugged. "Dunno. Some kind of commotion at the gates, security's being tightened inside. Andavista says jump, I reckon it's our job to ask which cliff he had in mind."

Brax stood silent for a moment, thinking. "Ro, go find Andavista or Saree and get it in person. No offense," she added to the two quads in front of her.

"None taken," their leader said; and then her sword was out and coming down on Brax. She struck hard and fast, but Brax was already under her arm and pushing her off center, taking only enough time to break the other woman's arm as she went down. The other seven moved in, Brax scrambled up with blood on her sword, and then they were on us.

I wasn't ready for the noise of it, the clattering of metal on metal, the yells, the way that everything reverberated in the closed space of the hallway. I could hear bolts slamming into place in the doors behind us, and knew that at least someone was alerted: no one but Andavista or Gerlain would get inside now. Lucky was shouting but I couldn't tell what or who it was meant for. Then I saw Ro shaking his head even as he turned and cut another soldier's feet out from under him, and I understood. "Go on," I yelled. "Get help! We don't know how many more there might be!"

For a moment Ro looked terribly young. Then his face set, and he turned up the hall. It was bad strategy on the part of the assassins to arrive in a group, rather than splitting up and approaching from both directions; but they'd had to preserve the illusion of being ordered to the post. Two of them tried to head Ro off: he gutted one and kept going, and Brax stepped in front of the other. Three horrible moments later she made a rough, rattling sound and they both went down in a boneless tumble. Brax left a broad smear of blood on the wall behind her as she fell.

Lucky and I were side by side now, facing the four that were still standing. Out of the side of my right eye I could see Brax lying limp against the wall. Lucky was panting. There was a moment of silence in the hall; we all looked at each other, as if we'd suddenly found ourselves doing something unexpected and someone had stopped to ask, *What now?*

"Blow them down," I told Lucky, and we swirled into them like the lightning and the wind.

I'd never before fought for my life or another's. These people weren't Tom; I couldn't drop my sword and call *stop*. And these were our own we were facing, people we'd eaten with, insulted and argued with, and whose measure we had taken on the training field. Some of them were people I had taught, muscle to muscle, skin to skin. Now I reached for them in rage, and my touch was voracious. I went in close to one, up near his center, my arm fully extended under his and lifting up, taking his balance, thrusting my weight forward to put him down. It was sweet to feel him scrabbling under my hands, pulling at my tunic, trying to right himself, and then my sword was at his neck and I cut off his life in a ragged line. His trousers soiled with shit and he fell into a puddle at my feet. My body sang. I took the taste of his death between my teeth and stepped on his stomach to get to the woman behind him.

I woke in our rooms. Ro was there, watching over me.

"How are you?"

"Don't touch me," I said.

He waited. "Brax and Lucky are going to be fine." I put a hand up to my head. "It was deep, to the bone, but it's not infected. They had to shave your head," he added, too late.

"Saree came around. Those two quads were hired to win a place in the guards and wait for the right moment. The one they took alive didn't last long enough to tell them who did the hiring. Poor bastard."

I felt empty and dirty, and I couldn't think of anything to say.

He swallowed, moved closer, but he was careful not to touch me. "Mars, I know it's the first time you've killed. It's hard, but we've all been through it. We can help you, if you'll let us."

"You don't understand," I said.

"I do, truly." He was so earnest. "I remember——"

I held up a hand. "Blessing on you, Ro, but it's not the killing, it's——I can't. I can't talk about it." I swung my legs off the other side of the bed, stood shakily, looked around for something to wear. My head hurt all the way down to my feet, but I wasn't as weak as I'd expected to be. Good. I found my tunic and overshirt, and a pair of dirty leggings.

"Where are you going?"

"I need to get out. I'll be fine," I added, seeing his face. "I won't leave the palace. I just want some time to think. I'm not looking for a ledge to jump off."

He managed a tight smile. I did not come close to him as I left.

I really did want to wander: to get lost. I had the wit to stay away from the public halls, and I did not want the company and the avid questions of other guards, so I steered toward the lower floors: the kitchens, the pantry, and the enclosed food gardens. I found a stair down from the scullery that led to a vast series of storerooms, smoke-rooms, wine cellars.

I thought about the killing.

The sword work wasn't so bad. The sensations of weapon contact were always more muted for me than hand-to-hand. But stormfighting was so much more intense: seducing my opponent into me, or thrusting myself into her space, or breathing in the smell of him while my hands turned him to my will. I'd got used to it being delicious, smooth, powerful, like gulping a mug of warm cream on a cold night. Until the hallway, until the man's throat spilled open under my sword, until I broke his partner open with my hands. With my hands—and the fizzing thrill through my body was overrun by something that felt like chunks of fire, like vomit in my veins. I hated it. It made me feel lonely in a way I'd never thought to feel again. So I sat in the cellars of the palace and wept for something I'd lost; and then I wept some more for the greater loss to come.

My head hurt worse when I'd run dry of tears. I gathered myself up and went to find my quad.

They were sitting quietly when I came into the room: Brax on one of the beds drowsing in the last of the sun through the west window, Lucky crowded beside her with her bad leg propped on a pillow, Ro on the floor nearby leaning against the mattress so that his head was close to theirs.

"Ho, Mars," Lucky said gently.

They were so beautiful that for a handful of moments I could only look at them. When I opened my mouth I had no idea what might come out of it.

"I love you all so much," I said. I wasn't nervous anymore; it was time they knew me, and whatever happened next I would always have this picture of them, and the muscle-deep memory of all our times.

"Being with you three is like… Gods, sometimes I imagine leaving home a day earlier or later. How easy it would have been to miss you on the road. What if I'd missed you? What would I be now?"

They were silent, watching me. I was the center of the world.

"That time on the road, when you asked me to…" I made a hapless sort of gesture, and Ro smiled. "You thought I was saying no, but what I was really saying was no, not like that." I swallowed. I wasn't sure how to say the next bit; and then Brax surprised me.

"The night before the guard trials, out behind the inn, when I thought we were practicing. We were really fucking, your way."

I felt like a lightning-struck tree, all soft pulp suddenly exposed to the world, ruptured and raw. And I did the thing more frightening than fighting Tom, or leaving home, or losing Ad. I whispered *yes*. Then I crossed my arms to hold myself in, and tried to find words to hold off the moment when they would send me away. "I didn't know until I met you on the road, and we began to practice, and every time we touched in this particular way I thought I would die from it. That's when I figured it out, you know. I was a virgin when I met you," and I couldn't help but smile, because it was so right. "For me, the touch of your palm on my wrist is the same as any act of love; it's my way of bringing our bodies together. It's no different from putting ourselves inside each other."

"Mars, it's—" Ro began.

"Don't you tell me it's okay!" I cut him off. "You're always the peacemaker, Ro, but you don't understand. You don't understand what I've done. Every time we've touched as fighters, all the teaching and the practice, it's all been sex for me, hours and hours of it with one of you or all of you, or other quads that we've taught. And you never knew. What's that but some kind of rape? It's bad enough with people I love, and then there's all those strangers. I've probably had more partners than all the whores in Ziren Square. And I can't help it, and gods know I can't stop because it's the most unbelievable...but what I did to all of you, that's unforgivable, but I was so afraid that you'd...well, I expect you can guess what I thought, and I'm sure you're thinking it now. No, wait," I said, to stop Brax from speaking. "Then there's this killing. You were right, Ro, I've never killed before, and it was horrible, it was disgusting because I still felt it even when I was pulling her arm out of its socket. And I didn't want to, I didn't want to, but I thought of what they'd done to Brax and then I was glad to hurt them and then there was this fierce, terrible wave... Oh, gods, I'm sorry." I was panting now, clenching myself. "I'm sorry. But it's there, and I thought you should know." They were still silent; Brax and Lucky were holding hands so tightly that I could see their fingers going white, and Ro looked sad and patient. "I love you," I said, and then everything was beyond bearing, and I had to leave.

⟶

I went back to the cellars because I didn't know where else to go. I did not belong anywhere now. I sat curled for hours next to one of the beer vats, numb and quiet, until I heard the chattering voices of cooking staff come to fetch a barrel for supper: I did not want to meet anyone, so I un-kinked myself and went farther down the hallway until I found a small heavy door slightly ajar, old but with freshly oiled hinges that made no sound as I slid through.

I came into a vast, dim place, heavy with green and the smell of water. Not a garden: an enormous twilight conservatory in the guts of the oldest part of the palace. Even through my despair I could see the marvel of the place, feel its mystery. There were trees standing forty feet tall in porcelain tubs as big as our room upstairs. Light seeped through narrow windows above the treetops. There were wooden frames thick with ivy that bloomed in lightly perfumed purple and orange and blue. Everything felt old and unused, sliding toward ruin, with the particular heavy beauty of a rotting temple. The humid air, the taste of jasmine on my tongue, the stone walls that I could sense although I could not see them under so much green—everything collided inside me and mixed with my own madness to make me feel wild, curious, adrenalized as if I'd eaten too many of the dried granzi leaves that Brax liked to indulge in sometimes when we were off duty. The narrow path that twisted off between the potted trees was laid in the unmistakable patterns of desert tile. I followed the colors toward the sound of rain, and the sound turned into a fountain, a flat-bottomed circle lined with more bright tiles. Strings of water fell into it from a dozen ducts in the ceiling high overhead, onto the pool and the upraised face of the woman in it.

She was dancing. From the look of her, she'd been at it a while: her hair was flung in sodden ropes against her dark skin, and the tips of her fingers were wrinkled, paler than the rest of her when she reached up to grasp at the droplets in the air. She breathed in the hard, shallow gasps of someone who has taken her body almost as far as it can go. Her eyes were rolled up, showing white, and her mouth hung half-open. She whirled and kicked to a rhythm that pounded through her so strongly I could feel it as a backbeat to the juddering of my heart. Faster, faster she turned, and the water turned with her and flung itself back into the pool. I knew what I was seeing. It was more than a dance, it was a transportation, a transmigration, as if she could take the whole world into herself if she only reached a little higher, if she only turned once more. I knew how it must feel within her, burning, building, until her body shuddered one final time and she shouted, her head still back and her arms clawed up as if she would seize the ceiling and pull it down upon her. Her eyes opened, bright blue against the brown. She saw me as she fell.

Bless her, I thought, *at least I'm not that alone.*

Her shout still echoed around the chamber, or at least I could still hear it in my head; but she was silent, lying on her side in the water, blue eyes watching me. I eased myself down onto one of the tiled benches bordering the walkway, to show I was not a threat or an idle gawper. There was a shawl bundled at the other end of the bench, and I was careful not to touch it. After a minute she rolled onto her back in the shallow pool and turned her blue gaze up to the high windows. Neither of us spoke. I was relaxed and completely attentive to everything she did: a breath drawn, a finger moved, a lick at a drop of water caught on her lip. When she finally pulled herself up to her knees, I was there with the shawl and an arm to help her raise herself the rest of the way. She draped the shawl around her shoulders but did not try to cover herself; she seemed unaware of being naked and wet with a stranger. I stood back when she stepped out of the pool.

She looked me up and down. She was medium tall, older by a few years, whip-thin with oversized calf muscles and strong biceps. An old scar ran along one rib. The skin on her hands was rough. I pictured her in one of the kitchens, or perhaps tending the smokehouse where the sides of beef and boar had to be raised onto their high hooks.

"I hope you closed the door behind you," she said absently, in a dry and crackly voice.

"The door? Oh…yes, it's closed. No one will come in."

"You did."

"Yes. But no one else will come."

"They might."

"I won't let them."

She looked me up and down. "You're a guard," she said.

"Yes."

"So you'd kill anyone who tried to get in."

"I'd meet them at the door and send them on their way. If they tried to come in further, I'd stop them."

She drew a wrinkled finger across her throat.

"Not necessarily," I replied. "I might not have to kill them."

"Oh," she said. "I would. I wouldn't know how to stop them any other way. I don't know much about the middle ground."

She had begun to shake very slightly. "You're cold," I said, and pulled off my overshirt to offer her. She peered at it carefully before she put it on, dropping the shawl without a glance onto the wet floor.

"Most people don't talk to me," she said.

"I'll talk with you whenever you like," I said, thinking that I knew very well how people would treat her, particularly if she wandered up to the kitchens with one of the meat cleavers in her hand and tried to have this kind of conversation. Standing with her in the dim damp of the room felt like being in one of those in-between moments of an epic poem, where everyone takes a stanza or two to gather their breath before the next impossible task.

She appeared to be thinking, and I was in no hurry. Then she straightened the shirt around her and said, "Walk me back."

"Of course," I answered. I plucked her shawl out of the muck and fell in behind her with my hand on my sword, the way I'd been taught. She was so odd and formal, like a little chick covered in bristles: she wanted looking after. When we left the room, she watched to make sure that I closed the door firmly, then nodded as if satisfied and led me back up through the cellars. I was surprised when she bypassed the carvery and the scullery, and nervous when she took the stairs away from the kitchen, up toward the residential levels of the palace: I wasn't sure what to do if someone challenged us, and I did not want trouble with Andavista on top of the mess I'd already made with my quad. But she held her head high and kept going, and then we made a turn and almost ran into Saree talking something out with one of his seconds. *Oh icy hell*, I thought, and was absolutely astonished when Saree gave me an unreadable look and then bent his head. "Prince," he said, and she sailed by him like a great ship past a dinghy, trailing me behind. As I passed, Saree pointed his finger at himself emphatically, and I nodded, and then followed the prince.

We came to the great wooden doors of the royal suite, and the four guards there stiffened. They opened the doors clumsily, trying to see everything without appearing to look at us, and I knew the stories would start a minute after the watch changed when the four of them could get down to the commissary.

The hallway was a riot of rich colored tapestries, plants, paintings, a table stacked high with dusty books: and silent as a tomb. I wondered if the king was behind one of the many doors we passed. A servant came out of a room at the far end and hurried toward us with a muffled exclamation. The prince waved her off, and I handed the servant the shawl as she stepped back to let us pass. Then the prince stopped in front of one of the doors and turned to me. Her eyes were hard, like blue stained glass. I saluted and bowed.

"You saw me," she said, and her voice was like her eyes.

I imagined what it would be like to practice with my quad from now on, their knowing what it meant to me every time we touched, their distaste or their tolerance, my most private self on public display because I had not kept my secret. I understood how she might feel; and she deserved the truth.

"You were beautiful," I said. "You were like a storm."

She looked at me for a moment, then she took in a breath and blew it out again with the noise that children make when they pretend to be the wind. Her breath smelled like salt and oranges. The door shut between us.

"What happened?" Saree growled when I found him.

"The prince asked me to escort her back to her rooms," I said evenly.

"Where did you find her? Her servants have been looking for her for hours."

"In the hallway near the armory." It was the farthest place from the cellars I could think of.

"Oh, really?" he rumbled. "She just happened to appear in the armory hallway soaking wet and there you were?"

"Yessir," I answered. "Honestly, sir, I didn't even know who she was until we met you. I just didn't think that she should be—I mean—"

He relaxed. "I know what you mean, no need to say any more. But we'd like to know where she disappears to." I stayed quiet, and he lost interest in me. "Don't you have somewhere to be?" he said, and I saluted and got out of his sight as quickly as I could. My head was too stuffed full of tangled thoughts to make sense of anything, and I didn't want to deal with Ro and Lucky and Brax until I felt clear. I took myself off into Lemon City for a long walk and did, in the end, get my wish: I got lost.

It was late when I came back to our rooms. The quad was there, and so was Andavista. They all wore the most peculiar expressions: Lucky was trying to send me seventeen different messages with eyes and body language, but all I got was the general impression that a lot had been going on while I'd been away. Then I looked beyond her, and saw the carrybags we'd brought with us all the way from the crossroads, packed now and waiting to be closed up.

"No, you idiot," Brax said. "Your things are in there too, we're being transferred. Don't look at me like that; everyone knows what you're thinking, we can always tell."

"Um," I said helplessly, and Ro grinned. Andavista stood up from where he'd been sitting, in our only chair. "Very touching. Sort it out later. You, I've just about run out of patience waiting for you, but I've got direct orders to fetch you all personally. I suppose I can be thankful you didn't decide to stay out all night. Particularly since this lot wouldn't say where you could be found." He squinted at me. "Well, at least you're not stupid enough to turn up drunk. Now, all of you, get your things and follow me."

He stomped out of the room and we scrambled to shoulder our gear and follow him. I shooed Lucky out of the way and picked up our biggest pack. "Get away from that, you can't carry it with your leg." She grimaced impatiently. "What's going on?" I whispered.

"You tell me," she whispered back. "All we got is some wild story at dinner about you and the prince, and then Andavista saying he's giving us a new home and everyone who's not on watch finding an excuse to wander by our rooms and goggle at us."

"Shut up and move," Andavista snarled without turning, so we did, Ro and I carrying everything between us while Brax braced Lucky with her good arm. Of course I knew where we must be going, but I could scarcely credit it: I'd only been nice, and certainly more free in my manner than what was due to her. But I was right: we went through the by-now-familiar wooden doors and into a room just beyond, where sleepy-eyed servants were busily beating the dust out of a rug and several coverlets, with a new fire in the hearth and a pitcher of mulled wine on a mostly-clean table. And my overshirt, carefully folded on the mantel.

Andavista said, "You've been assigned as the prince's personal guard. You're with her wherever she goes, all of you, which means more time on duty than before. She breakfasts at midmorning, you two—" looking at me and Ro, "—report to her then. If she forgets to let you out for meals, let me know. I expect a full report every day from one of you, personally to either me or Saree, no exceptions. You'll go back to teaching when you're all off the sick list, at least until you've got others good enough to take over. Where you find the time is your problem. And don't get above yourselves, I'll be watching. And don't let so much as a mouse near her," he added, in a different tone. Then he glared around the room and left. The servants scuttled out behind him.

My three pounced on me with questions before the door was closed. "Wait, wait," I said, trying to gather my wits while Ro poured us a cup of wine. Between hot swallows, I told them about meeting the prince, curiously content even though we all knew why I'd been downcellar in the first place, the unfinished business between us.

"Unbelievable," Lucky said. "How do you do it, Mars?"

Brax said, "I wouldn't go planting any gardens here, Luck. She's thrown out more guards than we have ancestors. She could change her mind anytime."

"I don't think so," I said. "She's never taken a personal guard before that I know of, just the shift watches outside the door. Can you imagine some of our mates in the barracks standing outside the conservatory doors while she... She'd have been a laughingstock years ago."

"So why now?" Ro said.

"I understand her." They looked at me. "Maybe I'm mad, too, I don't know, but seeing her dance—you know what I think? I think she wants someone to share with. I told her she was beautiful, and she was. Maybe no one else ever has. But whatever you think of her, you mustn't—you mustn't hurt her."

"Oh, Mars," Lucky said sadly. "Of course we won't."

"I know, I'm sorry. It's just—"

"We know what it is," Ro said. "And we decided we don't want to talk about it until you and Lucky and Brax are better. And that's the end of it," he said as I opened my mouth to speak. "Now, who gets the bed nearest the fire?"

We and the prince began getting used to each other. She spent a lot of time watching us; it was a bit unnerving at first. She tested us in little ways. She led us on some incredible expeditions into the belly of the palace. She seemed more and more trusting of us; but she did not dance. She seemed to be waiting for something.

And so was I. Every arc of motion that returned to Brax's arm was one step closer to all my worst fears. By unspoken agreement, we did not practice, and the others stopped making love in front of me. There was a particular kind of tension between us that I could not define, that made me miserable when I let myself think about what it all might mean, and what I had to lose. I wondered if the prince felt it and thought it was directed at her: it made me try even harder to be easy and gentle with her, who'd had so much less than I.

Ro and I came back to our rooms one night to find Lucky and Brax already toasting each other with a mug of beer from a barrel swiped on our last trip to the cellars. "Back on duty tomorrow," Lucky grinned around a mouthful of foam. "Hoo hoo!" She poured, and we all drank. I felt numb.

"Oh, sweet Mars," Ro said, "don't look like that. Don't you know we see right through you?" Then he took my cup away and opened his arms and folded me into himself, and Lucky and Brax were behind me, gathering me in, stripping off my clothes and theirs. "I don't know if I can—" I began to say, and Brax murmured, "Shut up, Mars." Then Ro shifted his weight and sent me down into Brax's waiting arms, and she pinned me for a lightning second while she brushed her breast against my mouth, and then rolled us so that I was on top and Ro's arms came around me in a lock, and I hesitated and he whispered *Go on* and I turned the way we'd taught ourselves and felt his thigh slide across my back and heard his breath hitch, and mine hitched too. And then it was Lucky with her leg across mine, strength to strength, my heart beating faster and faster, everything a blue-heat fire from my groin to the tips of my fingers. They traded me back and forth like that for some endless time, and each moment that they controlled me they would take some pleasure for themselves, a tongue in my mouth or a wristlock that placed my hand on some part of them that would make them moan; and I moaned too, and then answered their technique with one of my own and changed the dance. Then Brax reached for Ro, and Lucky and I continued while beyond us they brought each other to shouts; and then Lucky was gone to Brax and it was Ro with me, whispering *Best me if you can*, and then Brax with her strong arms; until finally the world stopped shuddering and we lay in a heap together in front of the fire. And later some of us cried, and were comforted.

~⊱

We are the prince's guard. When she sits in a tower window and sings endless songs to the seabirds, we are at the door. When she roams the hallways at night peering through keyholes, we are the shadows that fly at her shoulder. She dances for us now, and we protect her from prying eyes; and when she is ecstatic and spent, when she is lucid and can find some measure of peace, we take her back to her rooms and talk of the world, of the rainbow-painted roofs of Hunemoth and the way that cheese is made in Shortline. She is safer now; she has us to see her as she is, and love her.

And there is still time for ourselves, to teach, to learn, to gossip with other guards and steal currant buns from our favorite cook. Sometimes the prince sends us off to Lemon City for a day, to collect fallen feathers from the road or strings of desert beads from the market; to bring back descriptions of her beggars and smiths and shopkeepers; to gather travelers' stories from the inns. Sometimes we carry home a flagon of spicy Marhai wine, and when she sleeps, we drink and trade wild stories until the moon is down. Sometimes we sleep cuddled like puppies in our blankets. Sometimes we fight.

Somewhere Down the Diamondback Road

A nd oh the feel of the road through the wheels and the carapace and the burnished bones of the machine that grit-slung us down the black-top. The road was a king snake with a long white back-stripe, and it whipped underneath us as we grab grab grabbed for the head, shooting upward, rolling off to the side and the rest stop sign and the gravel beyond as I stroked the wheel and broke the neck of the spin. Then the road lay dead and cooling under us, and the air burst in like a snatching arm when Billy opened the door and laughed Jesus Christ Carol Ann and fell out dizzy.

Liberdad Joe rolled past head back victory-grinning and flashed down the road with the other cars into the sun and the memory of the race. Sweat ran down my insteps and pooled in the heels of my boots, brown leather and diamondback skin, arrows pointing down on the clutch, down on the gas, down on the pavement as I stepped out, looked at Billy leaning against the tire, trembling spent from the whoops of our carnival moment, Billy the only one who has ever kept up with me and I smiled.

I drove in the morning. Billy didn't drive, no interest in outstyle skills he said but there is nothing outoftouch about the rhythm of rubber on heat-slick asphalt that is my best freedom left. Billy loved to fly but not for the Authority never he never we all said and they put him on the road grounded him me all of us like the cliptailed canaries in cages at the Waste Management Center that once I tried to set free. Now Billy was a passenger and I had a one-arm tan and a view of the left side of his face, good view, pretty face, that square jaw and the silveryellow hair folded on his head like bird-wings at rest, the hair so soft to smear back from heavy cheekbones and the jaw all knotted muscles and hot mouth, Billy taught me how we all drive in our own way. And what roads we take.

"There's a hitcher up there, Carol Ann, can't we stop?"

"There's two hitchers and only one is my size. Bad odds, lambchop."

Dunno how he made that sulky-cheeked look hit me like it did, he never even turned my way. Lost my concentration, that cocoon of speedmotion that makes driving the road just like rubbing your finger down the bone of your own thigh. Slowed down for a look at the hitchers, one grown one not, the young one so fresh and fuzzysoft in the bright bright sun, clearly only two minutes on the road and helpless as hell, learn to take care of yourself first Billy. But of course we don't know how we haven't learned, that's why we're here and Authority takes care of us now.

Billy-boy swallowed. "Never mind." And oh I thought, look at the other there: older, ancient snake-eyes. So familiar, those eyes had seen around some corners of mine, raw places that wailed oh no not again and I tried to drive by, Billy said try Carol Ann try and I wanted to disappear down the throat of the road into the horizon, wanted to just keep going right on by but my boot-toe slapped the pedal no and the brake pads bit oh no and hissed us to a stop.

"Mason."

Such a happy smile. "Carol Ann. A pleasure to see you as always."

Point for Mason. He and Billy squared off in tiny ways, shoulders and snorts like they always did, Billy so calm so careful of whatever the road brought us and Mason silent and sharp like the wrist-knives I wore, Mason always looking for the latest twist. I took a closer look at the latest twistee squinting at me, eyes toward the sun. And back to Mason, watching me watch her, smiling.

"Cute," I said. "What's this?"

"This is Jenny." Just a baby, brand new, still scrubbed from the last real bath they gave her, shiny and tousled and so like me that I reached for her but she cringed away. How did she fail I wondered, where did she run from that brought her to this moment in my sun? Time ago I could have been this wide-eyed child and she saw it too, said what is this, Mason? Oh it's only me I almost told her, you're only me fresh out on the road first time, so many years ahead of you in the dust of yourself. Oh no, beautiful child.

Mason gave me time for one more good look then moved toward me with something in his hand, glass and needle poison sac, and Billy long-stepped between us and Jenny stood back trembling with nowhere to run.

"Billy."

"No, I won't let you, not again Mason, don't you know what it'll do to her? It took me long enough to put her back together from the last time, why can't you just leave us alone? Let them get someone else. You can tell them to get someone else. Why does it always have to be her?"

"She's the one they need. What a good example she would be..." He almost touched my cheek. "But she's tough," with such regret, I always loved Mason for that. And they looked at me, muscles fluttering under skin warm and tight where the adrenaline blood rushed in, just as scared as Jenny, as all the littleones in that warm dim room of the Center after the vans brought them arms still bruised where mommydaddy tried to clutch them back. Why did we let ourselves go? "I think you've lost your perspective, Billy," Mason said and moved fast and the glass snake slithered toward me sank its juices deep and put ice across the backs of my eyes and into my palms. I thought of all the small soft faces close your eyes and I'll tell you a story I said and Mason moved back and there was Jenny, Jen–nee, the name rolled off my tongue like the warm oil in the guts of the car that stood engine ticking as it cooled and I thought I was an engine racing down the road, not the driver anymore only the machine. Jenny rolled her eyes up at me under their lashes, she moved no not quite moved, she leaned in toward Mason and I thought no help for you there sugarplum. Oh, they sent me one so young.

Moving in, a long step away now. "How old are you, darlin?"

No she didn't like that at all, saw her bridle and those little muscles in her neck stiffen but she answered, "Sixteen."

"Sixteen," and for a ghost moment there was music, the smell of young skin, the humid feel of just-ended laughter in the air, all wrapped around sixteen when I was only me myself and there was no new Authority to swallow me whole and all the future was open and free. But the road rolled over me and left me with the still- ness of the children as the gas slid sidewinding down their sleeping throats while they dreamed of the once-upon- a-time place where it was always summer and everyone belonged, why why why I asked and Director said twenty more tomorrow our new world ten more tomorrow not our kind fifteen eighteen mustn't question Authority hun- dreds more better off this way but I knew I knew and one tomorrow a child opened her eyes as the gas bit into her brain and she was me as different as I was no different at all. And I opened the doors and said run run run and I ran too but not fast enough. Never fast enough and they put me on the road fast faster my heart and Billy said, "God Carol Ann no," and Mason said nothing and oh yes I said as I flexed my wrists back sharp and the long handles shot out of the sheaths underneath, and I split my fingers around the thin metal and pressured the spring switch to snap out the triangular blades, little fangs, and fisted the knives to show Jennybelle. Her mouth slacked open and the whites showed all round those blue eyes, summertime eyes. Your eyes will return in forget-me-nots, in the wild- flowerings of a much better place than this, I told her, and then I was deep-breathing head back in tears for the won- der of those eyes and the place I would send her. My fists came forward wetsmacked into her sweet drawn navel just waiting to be filled and she oomphed as we connected and I drank her energy through the steel blades, we were close enough to kiss and I put the weight of my body in my boot across her foot held her rooted smiled and flexed my arms strong from wrestling with the road, flexed and red-ripped them away from each other one up one down, and she came apart in my hands. She twitched and scattered across the gravel. The road drank her in.

———

I had to drive with my forearms until we got to the next rest stop. Billy waited obedient, too quiet, for the maintenance crew to pick up my broken toy. Mason rode with me in Billy's seat, humming. Then we were in a cooltiled room with sink and seats and wallscreen and I held my arms out over the basin for soap and water, but Mason was there first to put more venom in my veins. I tried to squeeze it wash it out but I could already feel my arm warm like cotton wrapping me from the wrist up, shrouding me, taking the ice away and leaving only the kill and the memory and the red on my skin. The screen above the sink hissed into static noise then into a face, a little sweat above the eyebrows, lumpy nose, a thick neck and a white collar and then it smiled.

"Good afternoon, Carol Ann."

I looked down. Soap lathered pink in my palms.

"How are we today?" and I thought maybe if I pre-tended not to know but they never let you pretend. "I can't hear you, Voice. You're not there." Harder and harder to say as the second skin of the drug wrapped around me.

"Oh no, that won't do. That's not the right attitude, Carol Ann."

"Please, I don't want to talk to you right now." Soap slicked down into the basin. I leaned dizzy against the screen.

"Tell me about your adventure today."

Hands squeezed the sides of the sink. "You tell me, Jennevere was your little tethered goat, you're the one who gave her to me so young oh jesus," and I was off reeling sobbing against the screen, the medical snake-spit kept my mouth talking and they wanted to know how did it feel this time was it good will you be good now Carol Ann and I tried to say Carol Ann is gone I sent her away see her running down the drain, let her run run run; but you have to be in pieces to go that way and I'm still here. And I fought and fought, where was Billy I needed him and they knew but there's nothing fair in this war where they make me my own enemy and I remembered one time saying Voice, Voice you make me sick, and Voice said yes that's why we're here.

And then finally there was Mason in the door, across the floor, arms around me lowering me to the cot at the side of the room where I have sometimes slept before, please let this be the last time let them give me up give me back let me alone let me go.

⊷

But when I woke up nothing had changed. Mason sat on the floor against the tiles watching water drip slowly from a silver faucet where I had washed someone from my hands. Dust and shoeprints on the concrete floor. I wondered who had been there looking at me what they had done, where they took me that I would never remember having been. Last time I woke up like that I found the wrist knives with the just-think triggers plugged in.

Later the wall fuzzed again into phosphor dots, many faces. I closed my eyes tight.

"She's still not cooperating." Was it the same Voice or different, I could never tell. More Voices rattled behind it.

"...this is taking too long..."

"...most promising compound we have overall..."

"...higher dosage?"

"...with an increased instability factor? No, the whole point is no martyrs. They have to see her willing..."

"...the Authority, how are we going to explain..."

"...how is she doing, Mason?"

She's awake, Mason said, ask her yourself.

Ah, hmm, yes, they said. "How are you feeling, Carol Ann?"

"I feel fine," thick-tongued, stupid, hating it. "You should come around sometime and let me make you feel this good."

Mason smiles the private smile looking at the blank screen.

"What do they want, Mason?"

"They want you to be happy, Carol Ann, you know that."

No I say with my headshake, with my tight shoulders and my look away.

Mason looks at me so fondly so secure I want to cry but Carol Ann the babykiller never cries anymore. They will put me in my place even if they have to find it for me even if they have to make me fit. Mason fits but I don't blame him, I could never hurt Mason, he's the only thing I have, Mason and Billy and the far distances of the road.

"One day they'll send you back to what you were before only this time it will be wonderful. Isn't that what you want?"

No I shake my head again, I will never want to like it, never want to give away the speed and the long straight line of open space in the center of myself where there is room for everyone.

"But you will."

"No," I say with my voice this time, lucid and clear from the place in me too large for them to find. "I won't do that anymore."

"But you are doing it, sweetheart," he says and smiles, shows his teeth. "You did it just a little while ago. You do it so well these days." He lays his hand warm steady hard on the back of my neck. "It's all right. You can trust me. I only want to help you," he says, the kindest lie he knows.

"Make them stop," I say, and I still do not cry.

"I can't do that. I'm one of them, you know that too."

Later, where's Billy, I ask. They took him away Mason says, they don't think he's an appropriate stimulus for you at this point in the conditioning process. Which I guess means they didn't think he was good for me after all, my precious Bill, sweet William gone to wherever bad experiments go but oh we drove so well and the room darkens for a while, and when I look up again Mason is gone but there are the keys he has left like a message, the keys, the ticket into the pitch and yaw of the road and the fierce slipstream beauty of the moments between, when the needlemade madness coils on the far side of the watching screen, when the air is sweet through the open window as I drive, drive on the highway in my mind.

Dangerous Space

I liked Lillie's Place. Black walls. Wood floor stripped by a thousand ammoniac swabbings. Frat boys clacking eight-ball in the back room, *Whoa, nice one,* while in front their older brothers drank beer with weekend-Goth girlfriends who were starting to suspect that office work wasn't as temporary as they'd thought; who wore their raccoon eyes like the men wore their college rings, that subtle blend of pride and desperation. And at the tables on the raised stage-left border of the dance floor, the currently-at-liberty bass players, the basement-studio indie producers, the DJs, the roadies. The music people. Lillie saved those tables for us because bands like playing to their own kind.

"Heya, Mars," she said, and set down two pints of Stella Artois. To the woman with me: "Sorry, hon, I thought you were someone else. Beer okay?"

"Whatever Mars drinks is great."

Lillie's face never moved, but I knew her well: I saw the smile under the skin. "Okay," she said.

I said, "This is...."

"Karen," Karen said after a moment.

"Karen is a big fan of Artie Z," I said.

"Ah," Lillie said, and gave Karen a closer look. "Would you like some chips and salsa?" Lillie always tries to be nice to the ones she thinks might end up with Artie, since he never is.

"Sure," said Karen, bright with hope. She took a sip of beer and made a little face.

Lillie turned back to me. "So...seventeen states?"

"Fifteen," I said. "I took a couple nights off."

Lillie laughed and shook her head. Then added, as she saw Karen's look—*Can I be in on the joke, can I be in*— "I like to keep track of the hearts Mars breaks on tour."

Karen nodded and smiled with tight lips, and I felt for her. She didn't want to hear about road sex games when she might be four hours from the lead guitarist's hands sliding under her shirt.

"I'll bring you some peanuts, too," Lillie told her. Then she peered at me. "You here for Heroes?"

I gave a small nod. Lillie shook her head a different way, a *you know better* way.

I shrugged.

She said, "Noir's opening. Ever hear them?"

I shook my head.

"Ah," she said. She gave me a look. "I'll be back with those snacks."

"What was that about?" Karen asked when Lillie had gone.

"I have no idea," I said, but I thought I did. And so I drank my beer while Karen chattered, and when the stage spots came up I sat forward.

Lillie's low voice came over the PA. "Welcome to Lillie's, boys and girls. Tonight, all the way from LA to our very own stage, we're pleased to welcome Heroes for a special two-set night."

Cheers from the audience.

"But right now, give it up for Seattle's own Noir."

Polite applause as the band took the stage, and what flashed through me was *Oh hell, I thought she meant the music* as the singer stepped up to the mic and said, "Hello on a rainy Friday night, we're Noir" —and then it was the music too as the drummer brought down his sticks, the bass walked in, the guitar wailed an impossible chord, and the singer opened his mouth and took me apart and put me back together again and again and again.

Which is not how I ever talk about music. Not in the dreamtime after a late-night load-out, when people who are too tired to sleep speak in low voices of important things as the bus wheels *chunk kerchunk* us to the next arena; not to the still-flushed faces after the last *that was great* kiss, even the ones who have the wit to ask about the life rather than what the band is really like; not to Lucky, who's like my sister but would only slap my shoulder with her calloused hand and say *Jesus, Mars, go get laid.*

They think they know me. That I'm expert at what I do. That I walk both sides of the line, studio and live. That every venue knows my name. That I can drink a lot and still be polite at a 5 a.m. call. That I will help you find a drugstore in a strange city at midnight. That I'm willing if I must to break everything from your expectations to your bones. It's all true, but it's not the *who are you* of me. Some think I carry some old anger or great grief, but it's not the loss of something precious that drives me: it's the never having had. If I am anything, I am longing; and music is the one certain door into me. That's too private to lay out for people as if it were no more than *Show me yours and I'll show you mine.*

But here mine was, on a rainy Friday night on Lillie's stage: all of me in a stranger's mouth, the mouth and the music so beautiful I didn't know which made my stomach tight.

Lillie set down baskets of chips and peanuts. "Another round?" she said. I'd felt her watching me from the bar since the first note, but I'm good at face.

"Can I have something different?" Karen asked, startling me. I'd forgotten she was there. After a moment, I said, "What do you want?"

"Cranberry mojito?"

"Sure," Lillie said, and I thought how sad that the sum of anyone's wanting should be a cranberry mojito and an anonymous fuck with a mean-spirited man of middling talent.

Lillie turned to me. "So?" she said.

"He's amazing," I said.

A pause, and that subterranean flash of smile. "I meant, another beer?"

"Sure," I said. It didn't matter what she saw. I do music, not musicians; it's too small a world to avoid each other if things go horribly wrong, which they always do. These are artists, after all, human silos of heat and darkness and two-year-old *mommy, love me!* ego. Wanting them to be other than they are is a fool's game.

I put my professional ears on for a song or two. It was as bad as I thought, so I sighed and rolled my shoulders, and let the music take me. People were up and dancing. The band was tight and focused, trading grins, having fun. Then, during a bridge, the singer knelt before a young woman at the front of the stage. Held his mic aside and said something to her. Laughed at her response. And kissed her. The audience whooped, and the woman's eyes were shining when he lifted his mouth from hers. She glanced at a young man beside her and said something else to the singer.

He put the mic to her mouth. She said, "You're making my boyfriend jealous."

"We can't have that," the singer said, and leaned into the young man and thoroughly kissed him too. The man went red; the audience went wild; and the singer smiled and went back to his song. And when it was done, he said, "Heroes are up next. We're back at ten. Thank you very much," and the lights came up.

I blinked. I told Karen to save my seat. Then I threaded my way through the crowd around the console.

"You the sound guy?" I said.

"Busy," the sound guy said. She must have been older than she looked—Lillie had served her—but she worked the old PM5D like a child poking a strange bug with a stick to see if it was still alive.

I checked her settings. "Notch the vocals down a little in the mids, they need to come more forward."

"The fuck are you?" she said, without looking.

"I do some front of house," I said. I could see *Fuck off* build in her face, but she caught it and squashed it. Then looked at me for the first time and said, without much grace, "What do you suggest?"

Good for you, I thought. I approve of those who can suck it up when they need to: grace can be learned. "Center it here," I pointed, "and ride this range until you find that raspy edge in his voice when he's gone right down to the heart of the song. Pin it there and leave it alone."

She looked at the display. "Okay," she said.

"Thank you," said a voice behind me.

I turned. "You're welcome," I said. "You desperately need a better mix." And then, to the infant sound guy, "No offense."

"You're Mars," he said. The infant's eyes widened the slightest bit. "Lillie told me you were in the house. I'm Duncan Black."

An elongated moment of looking at each other, taking measure, taking time. Thirty-something face. Thousand-fathom eyes, that music swimming deep within them.

"I'll do your second set," I said, which was not at all what I'd intended.

"Good," he said.

We settled it over beer after the set, while Heroes did their best to give the crowd headaches.

"What about Jenny?" he said, with an indecipherable look toward the bar, where the infant was doing her best not to cry into her beer.

"I'll show her how to do a decent monitor mix. We'll see how it goes."

The look turned to me. "Why?"

"Someone has to teach her."

"She went to school."

"Please," I said. "Are we doing this, or not?"

"We're absolutely doing it," he said.

"Then I'll see you tomorrow," I said, and shoved my way to the bar to raise one finger to Lillie. As she pulled the tap on another beer, I said into Jenny's ear, "You want to be a real engineer someday?"

Sometime in the last minutes, she'd lost the crying fight. She bit her lip. Then wiped her swollen eyes and nodded.

"Okay," I said. "Welcome to boot camp. You're a woman, you have to work harder, deal with it. If you have to cry, keep stacking PA while you do it."

She took a breath. "Right," she said, and left her beer unfinished, and joined Noir's guitarist in carrying cases out the door. He gave her a raised eyebrow and an amp.

Lillie slid me my beer. "Did I see you with Duncan Black?" she said, as if she hadn't been paying fierce attention.

"Mmm," I said.

"They can't afford you."

"Oh, well," I said.

There was a pause as the sound of the music and the shove of the crowd swirled around us.

"I knew it," Lillie said, with the satisfied smile of someone who's finally got your number. "You're just another fucking romantic."

After Heroes wrapped, I took Karen to the green room. She was dry-mouthed and obviously wet at the other end, radiating pheromones and the excitement of a little girl who fears that any second now she'll wake up from the dream.

I nodded to Odi and Yazz as I passed. Odi ignored me, he always does, but Yazz put a sweaty hand on my arm and said, "Mars, let's find a corner and talk business."

I said, "I just climbed into bed with Noir. Maybe next year."

"Son of a bitch," he said. "I'm gonna kill that fucking Duncan Black. How about I double your rate?"

"You're a prince," I said. "How about I hook you up with someone good that maybe even Odi will like?"

Yazz snorted. "Whatever," he said. His face was still red from exertion, his hair wet, his t-shirt sticking to his barrel chest and ribs. He gave Karen an assessing look. "Who's your friend?"

Karen swallowed. "Karen, this is Yazz. Yazz, this is Karen. I promised to introduce her to Artie."

Yazz rolled his eyes. "Whatever," he said.

Across the room, Artie heard his name, or maybe he just smelled her, the way predators do. He turned a shark's eye toward us. Five minutes later, Karen was tucked like a round-eyed baby seal under his arm, and I was back out on the main floor. I gave Lillie a wave as I headed for the door.

"You deliver the package?" she asked.

"How's that for romantic?" I said.

I ate burgers with the band the next day at a bar and grill overlooking Pike Place Market. Below us, professionally jovial fishmongers tossed whole salmon back and forth over laughing tourists. From up here, you could see the occasional bit of fish flesh drop onto an unsuspecting head.

They were already squeezed into a booth when I arrived, halfway down their drinks, and I pretended not to understand that they'd met early to talk me over. I leaned across the table to shake hands, and then took the seat Duncan had left open beside him. The heat of his body made a warm space that I slid into easily. *I really should*

not do this, I thought, and smiled at the waitress and ordered iced tea.

Small talk about the show. Road stories. When Con
began to tap his fingers restlessly, I opened my bag and
brought out the CDs Duncan had sent home with me.

I'd spent the second half of the night losing sleep; the
first half I lost myself in Noir. So intimate, the 3 a.m.
charcoal stillness of the world and their music in my headphones. Con carrying us between his drumbeats. Angel's
bass the supple swaying spine of the song. Johnny, who has
found rapture in his guitar and has the sense not to hold
too tight. And Duncan passionate, smooth, rough, gentle,
hard between my ears because through headphones music becomes conversation, relationship, sex, confession.
Lifeline.

"This is what I hear," I said. "Your production is really clean."

Con started to grin, and I shook my head. "Too clean.
Hard plastic." He lost the grin as I went on, "You sound
like a bunch of twenty-year-old white boys."

He put his chin out.

"Did you produce?" I said. He didn't answer. "No offense," I said. "You've got amazing beats, and you're a
clean drummer, which you need to be because these guys
like to play dirty. So control the song, that's your job. But
not the sound."

Con looked unconvinced. Johnny stared out the window. Angel looked anxious. And although I did not look at
him, I could feel Duncan's interest and amusement and his
willingness to sit there all afternoon if that's what it took.

"Your live bootlegs trade well online?"

"Sure," Angel said.

"Website hits spike after a show? Downloads?"

Johnny nodded without looking away from the world outside.

"But your backlist doesn't move."

Now Johnny looked at me.

"Why do you think that is?" I said.

Con frowned. Took a breath. Said, "Okay, what do you suggest?"

It was unmistakable. I said, "Is Jenny your sister?"

He stared at me, and then he made a small sound that might have been a laugh and gave me a *go on, dispense wisdom* wave of his hand.

"Record analog," I said. Now I definitely had their attention. I grinned. "Have you ever?"

"No," Angel said, as if *analog* meant *naked*.

"But—" Con began.

"I like to put my hands on the music," I said. "You hear anyone say *Fix it in the mix*, run like hell. It's bullshit. You guys make real music, why dumb it down?"

Johnny leaned back against the booth and said, "Why are you doing this?"

I felt Duncan shift beside me to better see my face.

Johnny went on, "You can work with anyone. You're way out of our league."

"You're in the wrong league," I said. "Maybe I can help with that."

"Why?" Johnny said again.

I leaned forward. "You remember last night in the middle eight of, what's it called, 'Just Around The Corner,' Duncan held the note way beyond...and you didn't just roll the measure again like most people would. You stretched it so it built." I pulled my hands apart as if the music were taffy in them. "And when he fell off the note, you fell with him. Pretty amazing."

His eyes narrowed.

"I like amazing," I said. "And there's nothing you can do with music that I can't keep up with. I can make the audience *hear* you. I can put you so far inside them they'll have to dig you out with a spoon."

His raised eyebrow, my upturned hands: an entire conversation between us. "Look," I told the four of them. "I care about music, and yours is brilliant. But I've long passed the point where I have to beg for it, so you decide. You want me or not?"

Johnny sat back. Angel grinned. Con said, "We don't have to get this deep and shit all the time, do we?"

"Nope," I said.

Duncan said, "Is someone going to answer the question?"

I turned to look him full in the face. "You answer it."

"Oh, yes," he said, "I want you."

I learned fast that Duncan could say things like that— words knit in layers so that *You're hired* was also *I'm thinking right now about getting you naked*, with both meanings plain—and then do nothing more except enjoy the heat it added to even the most everyday moments. It wasn't his standard line in seduction: after shows, or in the clubs we frequented to hear other bands, he charmed in the facile rock-star way that made *sex with Duncan Black* a door prize, a luck that as a matter of course would be someone else's tomorrow. But anyone who became a long-term part of his creative world would find themselves at odd moments under the spotlight of a sexual attention that was riveting in both its force and its lack of expectation. We might sit across a pub table talking about compression or slimming down the rig, and suddenly he'd say something or just get that look and I'd be back in that moment, *Oh yes I want you*, his eyes full of music and sex, the band watching with varying degrees of *there he goes again* while I was rooted to my seat for a hard pair of heartbeats. And as he had done then, Duncan would watch and wait. All I had to do was smile slow, or laugh and shake my head, or give it right back to him, *Do you kiss your mamma with that mouth?* He'd smile, and we'd move on. He just needed to check the connection.

It's a good game if you have the stomach for it, if you enjoy the simmer of a rhythm like slow and endless chess. But if you began to boil, if you began to push, if you caught him in a dark corner and offered the endgame, you'd get it—he was always up for it—but the rest would disappear. I saw too many people who thought they were different carry the glow of great sex for a few days until, in public, the first apologetic look as he passed them by, the first hint of *You should have known it would turn out this way*. You could stay, but why? The creative spark was gone, crushed under the weight of wanting more. Not a trade I was willing to make. So I enjoyed the touches, the wordplay, how his singing hollowed me out, the music in his eyes. I played the game well. How much I sometimes burned in private was just the price of life in the funhouse.

And it was fun—stupid silly fun, deadly serious fun, everything in between. I let Yazz persuade me into accepting so much money for the eighteen-city second leg of Heroes' tour that I could then afford a long stretch of time in Seattle, taking a few studio gigs and giving the rest of my days and nights to Noir: two or three shows a month to learn their music live, and hours in my studio roughing it up as much as I could in remix, and persuading the band to re-record this and that. Analog. You would have thought I was asking them to kiss snakes.

I spent so much time inside the music that I began to feel it inside me: sliding under my skin, stretching in my muscles when I moved. Finding its way farther into me every time I put my hands on it. Knocking sometimes on my deepest doors. Startling, but not a problem: I haven't worked with music this long without learning to defend against it. Music is beautiful and cruel; it doesn't care what it makes you feel as long as it gets in. I put Noir so deep into audiences that I'm sure some went home unsettled by longing suddenly unlocked within them, some old dream let loose to burn or break again. What I do is not always a kindness: but it's my talent to hear the heart of a thing and make other people hear it too.

They did hear, more and more with every show. "Wow," Angel said one night in the green room, pouring beer down his throat so fast I don't think he tasted it, mopping sweat from his face with the one dry edge of the t-shirt he had just peeled off. "Wow. Look at them."

Them was a varied crowd of fans circling in slow currents through the backstage area; tattooed young men in motorcycle boots trading euphoric smiles with forty-year-old women in Manolos and Seven jeans. Wow, indeed. Duncan sat on a grungy sofa across the room; I caught his eye and tilted my head toward the scene. He grinned, nodded, and returned to charming the woman beside him, brilliant blue eyes and a *let's find out* smile, into an early departure.

"Excuse me," a voice said at my elbow. I turned. She was mid-twenties, combat-ready in layered shirts and cargo pants with enough pockets that she didn't need a purse. I made a private bet she had a toothbrush with her.

She looked at Johnny, who was busy being rumpled and poetic in a corner, and then at me. "Are you with the band?"

"Yes, I am," I said. "Would you like a drink?"

∾

In the dark of my bedroom, she propped herself on one elbow, her eyes glittering in refracted late-night city light.

"It must be amazing," she said. When they say it like that, they always mean life with the band, as if it were some combination of endless after-show parties, rampant sex, and midnight sing-alongs on the bus. The three-nights-on-two-nights-off grinding schedule, the set-up and tear-down of tons of equipment, the endless stupidity of vendors, missed meals, drunken fans who want to touch the pretty buttons on the board, throwing up in a strange parking lot before boarding the bus for a four-hundred mile drive in the sour smell of people who have chosen to sleep rather than shower, is never what they mean.

"It has its attractions," I told her, tracing the shadowed curve of her waist where it rose to her hip.

"Oh, sure. Sex, drugs, and rock and roll," she said with a laugh, and rolled onto her back under the pressure of my hand. They never understand. *Oh sure*, they say, the knowing nod, the serious mouth. *Oh sure*. And in their avid eyes I see them thinking it's the kind of dirty that always washes off, and they're dying for it.

She pulled me to her and wrapped one leg around me. She moved against me. She whispered in my ear, "So, what's Johnny really like?"

I agonized over the first album remix so much that Lucky, with whom I had dinner at least once a week, finally refused to feed me until I showed some fucking backbone. So I took the CD first to Con's small office in the pub he managed: he heard it through, shook his head, and said, "Well, fuck me." As the album played again, we talked about growing up in Iowa, the rhythm of train wheels that came across the fields into a young drummer's window at night. It made more sense of him for me; his steadiness, his preference for dealing with life at the ground level.

"Thanks for what you're doing for Jenny," he said as I left. "She likes you."

"Jenny's welcome," I said, and went to Angel next, at the earnestly Seattlesque credit union where he was a loan counselor.

"You look funny in a suit," I said.

"Blow me," he said cheerfully, making a multi-pierced teller snicker. He didn't have an office, so we sat in his car in the sun to listen, windows down, the music spreading its arms toward the high blue sky and very nearly reaching it. A bike messenger cutting through the parking lot slowed and then circled us round and round, listening.

"Well, fuck me," Angel said.

"Some great bass lines."

He grinned. "They're not so bad." And went back into the bank muttering *analog* and shaking his head.

And then to Johnny and Duncan at the apartment they shared; the top floor of an old lumber baron's mansion in Capitol Hill, beautifully renovated with, blessedly for neighbors, attention to soundproofing. They sprawled on the sofa, Johnny still in his waiter's apron from his lunch shift, Duncan on a day off from his erratic schedule of office temping and teaching piano. Duncan lay back with his head on Johnny's thigh as the music rolled out of their very nice speakers.

"Fuck me," Johnny said when it was done.

Duncan got that look and opened his mouth.

"Don't start," I said. "Do you guys know you talk like each other? I'm getting you all the t-shirt."

Duncan grinned. "It's fantastic, Mars, was what I was going to say."

"Blow me," I said. "Oh Christ, I'm doing it too." Duncan laughed, and even Johnny grinned as he reached for the remote. "Let's hear it again," he said.

F-tech was just coming into use around that time in the pharmaceutical industry: feeling technology that allowed researchers a first-hand experience of reactions in subjects testing new drugs—nausea, fatigue, the specific location of headache, all available through an adaptation of augmented cognition technology that mapped limbic brain activity and physiological sensation. It took some bright spark from marketing who didn't give a shit for the purity of science to realize the tech was a better product than any of the drugs it was helping to test. The company began marketing to doctors: instead of relying on the patient to fumble his way through metaphor or vague pointing, just put on the funny wire hat and for those few moments, make his experience your own. Feel your appendix swell inside you; share Alzheimer's dementia; find out what PMS is really like.

It took maybe a second and a half for the adult entertainment industry to get in on the game, and have some fun with the name F-tech, with dramatic results: since it was real-time tech that only worked with real live people, porn was out and peep shows were in—and everyone was curious to find out how the other half lived. How does it feel to be hard inside someone, to be tight and wet around them? It no longer took eleven inches or double-D to be a star: it took the ability to have your own kind of great sex—tender, enthusiastic, rough, whatever turned you on—in front of real people, to shudder and strain and come as hard as you could so they would too. No more faking: only the endless possibilities of human sensation. One enterprising journalist sought out women who'd never had an orgasm as volunteers, arranged a show, and wrote about it. Heartbreaking that there were so many candidates; fascinating to read about someone's most intimate awakening, and consider that such a private thing could now be a gift like season tickets or a bottle of wine.

Lucky, always curious, went to a show and came to our weekly dinner with her customary unflappable response to the world exploded by plugging into a man having sex with a woman. "I had no idea," she kept saying around mouthfuls of spaghetti. "No fucking idea. No pun intended. It's so *different* for men."

"You think?" I said. "And did you do the woman too?"

I grinned when she shrugged. She made a face and said, "It's fine for you, wander all over the playground if that's your thing. Me…." An internal conversation, another shrug. "Call me conservative. I don't do guys." She grinned and drank some wine. "But it sure was interesting to be one for an hour."

"Aren't you curious about straight sex?"

She snorted. "Been there, don't like it."

"Okay, but do you wonder how it feels to a woman who does?"

She snorted again, but she looked thoughtful as she attacked her spaghetti.

Later, she said, "You maybe want to go sometime?"

I shook my head.

She gave me a searching look. "Why not?"

Because I don't need to, is what I did not say. I know how the best sex feels. It feels like music.

It can be confusing when someone hands you something you've wanted fiercely. It's easy to transfer the hunger for the thing to a hunger for the person who gives it to you. Being on the road, sundered from the usual anchors to daily life, just makes it more easy. So I was waiting when we took our first roll through California, an eight-day hit-and-run of buzz venues I'd put together through my network; and after the gig at the Troubadour, Jenny turned to me as we were loading the van in the buttery warmth of the LA night and said, "Mars, it is just so *fantastic*." She was breathless and excited; the 'Sound Guy'

button I'd given her pulled down the top of her shirt just enough; and she gave me an impulsive full-body hug and looked up at me for a breath, two, until I said in a neutral voice, "I'd love to kiss you, Jen, but I can't afford to lose my monitor guy."

She blinked. "Oh," she said, "I——"

I winked.

"Oh, you were joking," she said.

"Can you hand me that case?" I said. And by the time she did, we were past the tricky part: tricky for me, too, because she was certainly my type, and it was intoxicating to feel her soft against me, to have her sigh in the way that means *All this for you.* I set my mouth into a smile and didn't let her see that I hadn't really been joking at all. And I simmered.

Later, I stood in a corner with an old friend, an engineer with boundless passion for heavy metal, the best I knew at riding the line just before people's ears actually began to bleed. Duncan came by, his eyes still swimming with music; it always took time after a show for it to seep out of him, the slow receding of an adrenaline tide. Whenever music was loose in him, he was more essentially Duncan: more wild, more charming, more intense, more physical, more willing to walk whatever edge he might find himself on. On nights of music, it was inevitable that his voice against my ear would make *You want me to bring you a beer?* feel like *You want me to bring you off so good you see stars?* But tonight I was worried about edges blurring. I shook him off, a little abruptly.

He gave me a quizzical look.

"You're interrupting my important sound guy talk," I said.

He rolled his eyes. "You going to introduce me?" he said.

"Go away," I said unconvincingly, and in the end it was I who went, pleading backache from loading the van, to stew alone in my hotel room about how fucking unfair it was that I had to keep saying no, no, no to the people I wanted most.

🕊

"You should have stayed for that beer," Duncan said the next morning on the phone, in the voice he reserved for significant news.

It was our one day off. "You woke me up," I said.

"Mmm," he said, and even over the phone I knew it meant *Well, not yet, but it's on my list.*

"Shut up," I said, my good humor at the game having apparently returned sometime during the little sleep I'd managed. "What did I miss?"

Con and I took a taxi to the restaurant. The others were waiting in the lobby, Johnny and Angel sharp-eyed and attentive as Duncan charmed the promoter.

"How are you, Jimmy?" I said.

"Mars, you look terrific," Jimmy Washington said. He gave me a one-arm hug with every appearance of warmth. "How long has it been?"

"Couple of years. Great to see you," I said, and Duncan quivered in silent amusement; on the phone, I'd said, *Oh Christ, watch your wallet and lock up your dog.* Still, Jimmy knew his job, and we can't all like each other.

"Great set last night," Jimmy said as the hostess led us to a window table. "Just great. We have got to get you out there." He spread his arm at the window toward the Great Beyond.

Nods all around. They were doing their best to be blasé, but I could sense the deep current of excitement running through them. I felt it too: I'd spent the week before the trip emailing mp3s to every promoter I knew; and even if Jimmy had the personal appeal of a sea slug, he was one of the best.

"Some acts, the trick is making people give a shit about the music. Not a problem for you. I got a niece at KCRW, she's gonna cream over your stuff and she knows everybody. We'll build audience, get some new work out in about...six months? Can you lay something down by then?"

Everyone looked at me. "I can if you can," I said to the band.

"Great," Jimmy said. "Then we'll slam a tour through the Top 20 markets about eight months from now. And I'm thinking a few opening gigs with an arena act in some of the mid-size markets." I could practically see him rubbing his hands together. "Maybe Superstition, maybe Ruff...we'll see whose schedule works out."

He sat back. The four of them exchanged looks.

"Let's do it," Johnny said, and reached across the table to shake Jimmy's hand.

"Great," Jimmy said, "just great. Draft contract in email tomorrow for your review. Let's get some champagne and talk strategy."

And so we did. It was good champagne; we got more. Eventually the talk turned tactical.

"We handle everything with the venue," Jimmy said. "We get you a contract tour manager who stays with you the entire run. You show up, do interviews or whatever, make the magic, get laid, we'll all make some money."

"Crew," Johnny said. "We want Mars at front of house."

I made sure my game face was on straight and lifted my champagne glass.

"We usually put together our own crew out of LA," Jimmy said. "That's how we like to work."

"Non-negotiable," Con said.

Jimmy's face didn't show much; he wasn't surprised, but he didn't like it. For one thing, it meant no skimping on logistics: I had a reputation for being prickly about hotel quality and people getting fed. Still, he knew the first rule of the road: he sucked it up.

"No problem," he said, and turned to me. "What're these guys paying you?"

"Usual rates," I said, without missing a beat.

"What, someone here is independently wealthy?"

"That would be me," Duncan said, with the smile that said *Call me a liar*.

Jimmy's face pinched briefly, as if he had a lemon in his mouth. Then he put the pro smile back on and said to me, "Well, it's not like you're not worth it."

"I'll bring my own monitor guy," I said. Con smiled.

"Okay," Jimmy said.

I said, "You open to tour manager suggestions?"

"Sure he is," Johnny said.

"Sure I am," said Jimmy, with a sigh.

"Mars, you *rock*," Lucky said after she got the call from Jimmy's people; then she morphed into a small whirlwind seemingly surgically attached to her cell phone, BlackBerry, fax machine, laptop, and bottomless quad latte. She was the best because she understood every job of every crew member on a tour, and because she was ruthlessly organized, endlessly inventive, and greeted every problem with the predatory cheer of an expert hunter who's just sighted something new to kill. She was at home with roadies and artists and promoters and VIPs; she simply made sure they all knew this was her tour, her artists, her crew. She ran a tight ship with a direct manner, an easy grin, an armful of spreadsheets, and an encyclopedic knowledge of the vagaries of venues from Seattle to Miami.

She knew the band, of course; anyone who became important in my life had to pass her inspection. She liked their music well enough, liked them. "Nice guys," she said early on, "but I don't really get the whole Duncan thing." Duncan, for his part, treated her with the detached courtesy he showed anyone who wasn't inside his creative or sexual space.

We all got together to talk tour. Lucky showed up at Duncan and Johnny's with an equipment rundown; a timetable to finalize the lighting design, rigging plan, and bus rental; a list of suggested clothes and personal items that would pack into a carry-on suitcase and cover almost every contingency; and a preliminary crew roster from Jimmy's office with personal comments on each candidate from someone Lucky trusted: "Except this guy," she said, "no one knows him, so I'm telling Jimmy tomorrow he's off the list." And she brought apple strudel.

"I love you," Angel said earnestly. "Please marry me and have my babies."

Lucky grinned. "I don't need babies," she said. "I have a band."

When we'd finished business and had moved on to trading war stories, Duncan produced a takeout menu. "There must now be Thai food," he said. He leaned over Lucky's chair with his arms on either side of her and held the menu open for her, his face next to hers. "Anything you want," he said.

She gave him a sideways look and said, "Okay, *tom kah* and a double order of ginger beef." And later, in a low-voiced kitchen conversation, she said with a small frown, "Was he hitting on me?"

"No, Luck," I said. "That's the thing he does. It just means you're in. If you don't like it, tell him."

"No, it's okay," she said. "It's weird, but..." She shrugged. "Artists." And that was it, as far as she was concerned. She started responding to him with variations of *Now, if you had a sister*, which seemed to delight him no end and was also a clear message. That was Lucky; very good with people.

Now that he could see the tour shaping up, the main chance on the horizon, Duncan began to work the new songs in earnest. That meant hours at the piano, or wandering around his apartment as if he might find lyrics in a corner, or being distracted at his current temp job by fragments of melody. "I can't even file when I'm like this. I forget the alphabet," he said one evening early in the process, when he was still talking to people.

I've seen plenty of artists at work. Music comes differently to them all. It's water from a tap they turn on and off at will; it's buried deep and they tear themselves bloody scratching it out; it's a box of tiny puzzle pieces they find at random over time and spend years fitting together. It's business as usual, it's agony, it's lust, it's crack, but it is never passive: only wannabes sit around waiting for songs to come in a box from UPS. I watched Duncan stalk and wrestle and seduce his music, I saw him struggle to give it voice, and I saw him for the first time truly volatile. I came to understand that music was a long passage to deep places that fascinated and compelled him, warm oceans of self that he could swim forever. Hard to leave. "He's got no end of songs in there," Johnny told me. "The trick is getting him to bring them back."

Duncan stopped seeing people. He barely answered email. Without warning, seemingly without regard, he disappeared into himself. The band was used to it. Lucky didn't care, as long as he surfaced briefly when decisions needed to be made. There was no steady lover to get prickly about being abandoned. And I became glad he was somewhere I couldn't really reach him, because it gave me time to deal with the fact that I missed him so much: that it wasn't just his music that was knocking at my door.

Lucky pried it out of me one night over a bottle of wine. "Jesus, Mars," she said in disgust. "Do not fall in love with a fucking musician."

"I knew you'd understand," I said.

"Jesus. Is this going to be a problem on the road?"

"It won't be a problem anywhere, Luck. He doesn't get horizontal with people he works with, and he doesn't fall in love with anyone. I'll get over it."

She gave me a look of absolute sympathy. Because it's all you can do: get over it. Let your tsunami of feeling foam itself out. Let the electric rush die because it's not convenient or not mutual or not worth the consequences in the cold morning after.

"Come on," she said, and handed me my jacket. "Let's go to Lillie's and get you laid. Maybe it'll help."

❦

D back with songs, Johnny's email said. *Will keep you posted.* I went to the kitchen and opened a bottle of Rioja, poured a glass, came back into the living room, and put Noir in my system. Let the wine and Duncan's voice warm me, and wondered where he wanted to take his music and whether the band would follow.

I've seen more groups fall apart over this in the long term than almost anything else, and small wonder: it's brutal. Someone drags up a bucket from the well that goes so deep in good artists and pours out the contents for other people to pick over, dissect, misunderstand, dismiss, or approve—and no matter what else, to change, even if only just by playing it enough to make it their own. Such a vulnerable thing; it takes skill and practice and a certain psychotic self-confidence to offer up handfuls of oneself again and again and again.

It also takes time to turn it into music—to work it through, play it out, fall in love with it, shape it to yourself. It's a band's most private process. So I was deeply surprised to get the phone call from Johnny two days later.

"Heya," he said. "If the studio's open any nights this week, we want to come in."

"Excuse me?" I said, and he laughed. "I know, it's insane. This stuff is amazing, Mars, you have to hear it. We want to work it out with you so we can lay it down rough if we feel like it."

"Okay," I said. "Come in tomorrow night." And I shook my head and started clearing my schedule.

It was good that I came in early to mic the space and fill the small refrigerator with the disgusting energy drinks that Con and Johnny lived on: because the band was early too. Angel, for whom lateness was a lifestyle choice, bounded in first with his bass and an enormous grin.

"So?" I said.

"Nope," he said. "Nope, nope, not a word, you just wait and see."

"Angel—"

"Nope."

Con was in next. I looked at my watch. "Just want to check the kit before we get started," he said.

"So?" I said.

He said, "Patience, grasshopper. We already talked about it, we don't want to give you any preconceptions."

"Hello," I said, "I'm your sound guy. It would be helpful to know what the sound is."

"Tonight you're the audience," he said. "Nobody else has heard this stuff, we want to make sure we're not all on dope about it."

I heard Johnny's voice outside. "...sit on it for the first chorus, and then the next time around," and he walked in with his head turned, "let it fucking go," his arm shooting music into the air behind him, toward Duncan.

"Great," Duncan said, and saw me, and grinned. He looked beautiful; tired and thin, but wearing the glow of hard work well done. He put his arm around my shoulders, pulled me close, briefly nuzzled my neck. "Mmm," he said, "you smell good," and I thought, *Oh fuck.*

He let me go, and fished a CD out of his bag; turned it between two fingertips. "Got something for you," he said.

"Promises, promises," I said, which got me a smile as well as the CD. I put it in the player and brought the remote to the small listening area in the control room. Duncan curled up at one end of the couch like a cat. I could feel him intent on me. That was fine; one of the necessary skills to work with musicians is staying relaxed under the laser gaze of an artist who's gauging to four decimal places your reaction to his work. I put on my sound guy face and settled in a chair in the listening pose, leaning back, head down, eyes unfocused.

It began: demo stuff, Duncan and the piano, the occasional drum loop. Two verses into the first track, the chorus came along and the song took a sudden, sexy turn; Duncan's voice roughened, and I could imagine the build of the drums, the erotic bass line, the urgent guitar...I looked up, astonished. They all broke into grins. "Isn't that the *shit?*" Angel said. "I was up half the night working out the bass."

"Wow," I said, and felt Duncan relax fractionally.

The rest were equally exciting. Songs about sex and love and separation. Stories of walking an edge and sometimes falling off. Roadmaps of perilous journeys into one's own soul or other people's arms. Simple songs about complicated things, by turns ferociously angry, desperately sad, fuck-me-now passionate, spiked with joy so sharp it almost hurt. They were raw, fractured, not yet whole; but the core of the music was there, waiting for the four of them to give it shape and make it Noir.

"Unbelievable," I said when it was done. And *Brilliant* and *Audio crack* and *That one will be everyone's breakup song*, and so on, because *great* is never good enough for the artists; they always want to know exactly what you mean and which nanosecond of the song you mean it about. Having answers is another of the skills.

"Let's do some work," Johnny said, and went into the recording room with Angel and Con to set up and tune.

Duncan stood and stretched and got himself a bottle of water. "I've been wondering what you'd think," he said.

"I think they're amazing," I said. "You know I like amazing."

He smiled; the artist's private smile, the power and pride when the work is good. "You know what's amazing?" he said. "I knew I couldn't write these songs. I knew it. And then I wrote them anyway."

I imagined him in the apartment finishing the last song, sitting still before it, drawing slow breath, smiling that smile.

"Now we find out if I can sing them," he said, and went to join his band.

So many nights working out the music until someone was too tired to keep up. So many marathon weekends. Life became a blur, hours of music running together like paint into strange patterns. It fascinated me to watch the dynamics among the four of them, to see revealed the core of a relationship closer and more complex than many marriages. Creative collaboration demands that some of our most well-defended barriers go down; and so I saw different facets of all of them, new vulnerabilities.

Some songs came together quickly; some were stubborn. We laid down hours of fragments and rough takes. They liked having ideas they could hear side by side: they spent hours back and forth between versions, closing gaps in interpretation and style, hammering out tempo and focus. Occasionally they would draw me into a discussion of how to balance the sound or how I'd apply technology to a particular musical issue; otherwise I tried to stay invisible in the control room. I was conscious of being in a delicate space, witness to a process I could disrupt if I were not careful.

Anytime they reached an *okay, let's try it* consensus, no matter how grudging, they'd play it. Some of the most interesting discoveries were in these *fine, whatever* moments, when someone who had been hanging onto a notion with both hands suddenly heard what someone else was talking about; and the act of making music became the act of changing a mind. It always came down to the music: what was good, and what made it better.

But that didn't make it easy. They had some terrible arguments. Con was mule-stubborn and turned red when he was upset. Johnny became excruciatingly reasonable, as if he'd found himself in the middle of an academic discussion rather than an intensely personal conflict about what makes a song work. Angel was impatient and flip, most so when he most cared. And I discovered that Duncan had a mean streak, a coldness that came out when he had to defend some aspect of the music that was twined too closely with his own psyche. He couldn't always separate art from self.

"Fucking cotton candy," Johnny said one night about a particularly elusive song. "This melody line is straight out of the eighties." He used the reasonable voice, as if it would mitigate the deadliness of the insult.

"Fuck you," Duncan said.

"We're not getting anywhere," Johnny said. That was certainly true; they'd been scratching their fingernails down this track for—I looked at the wall clock—four hours thirty-nine minutes this particular night, and it wasn't the first time.

"The melody's okay," Con said. "Well, it would be if it wasn't so slow. It's a rock song, let it rock."

"It's no fucking rock song," Angel said. "I don't know what it is anymore."

They had tried any number of approaches: ballad, full-out headbanger, most things in between. They had dragged the melody around the room until it was almost unrecognizable. They had kicked the stuffing out of the song.

Duncan looked furious and miserable when Angel said, "Maybe we should just let this one go, you know?"

Damn, I thought. There was something about the song that gave me shivers, even mutilated as it was now. I wanted them to make it work.

Johnny looked at me through the window. "What do you think, Mars?"

The others looked at me too, and I wondered if they were as surprised as I was. This wasn't a sound question; it was a music question.

I checked Duncan; his face was closed in the way that meant he'd left the realm of discussion and was well into the land of come out swinging. Not a place I wanted to go with him. But this song...I said, "I think there's something there, but that's up to you."

"You think it can work, tell us how," Con said.

"I'm not a musician," I said. "This is your turf."

Angel said, "Mars, stop fucking around and just tell us what you think."

Duncan said nothing.

"Give me a minute," I said, and rubbed the back of my neck; and opened my memory to all the variations they'd tried. My talent, to hear the heart of a thing: but now I heard nothing, and I thought again, *Damn*. And remembered him saying *I knew I couldn't do it and I did it anyway*. So I took a breath and tried to hear differently: I listened to my body's memory of when the song had made me pay attention, when it had scratched at the door of my most private self.

Oh, I thought, *oh*.

Walking into the recording room, I was the most nervous I've been in years around musicians. I squatted by Duncan's chair. He raised a cool eyebrow.

I said, "Can I see it?"

He regarded me for a moment and then handed me his working notebook, a sturdy composition book with a black and white checked cover. It was open to the song. I scanned the lyrics and then looked at Duncan. Gathered myself internally. "It's two different songs at once, is the problem," I said. "You walk right up to the real song and then back off."

Without moving a muscle, he went from cool to glacial.

I bypassed all the sunny phrases about the lover who is the treasure, and circled one section with my finger. "My opinion, this is it," I said. "You should start here and see where it goes."

"Let me see," Angel said, and took the notebook from my hands before I could turn it around to show Duncan. Con and Johnny crowded around Angel to read.

"Huh," Con said.

"Maybe," Angel said.

"Why?" Johnny asked me.

I said, "No matter what you do with the rest, this is the part I always hear." I put my hands on my body to show I meant *what gets in.*

Johnny gave the notebook back to Duncan and picked up his guitar. Duncan looked at me. I pointed again:

You shouldn't be in these private places
Down in the cellar of me
Where I am revealed
Where I am laid bare
Where my fears run like rats
And my longing stands naked

But I find you there
I keep finding you there

Better be careful
It isn't safe here
Not always what you expect it to be
The water is deep here, the ground is uncertain
It's dangerous space this far inside of me

Duncan's face went still.

Johnny picked out the first phrase of an edgy melody line, a sound like the air feels when storm clouds gather on the horizon.

"Huh," Con said. "Interesting."

"What do you think?" Johnny said to Duncan, and Duncan closed the notebook, threw it hard across the room, got up, and left the studio. He slammed the door. It sounded especially loud in the silence of our surprise.

After a moment, Angel said, "Here we go with the drama. I hate this part."

We waited. Duncan didn't come back. Johnny sighed and went after him. Returned alone; said, "He's walking home." Angel and Con exchanged looks and started packing up their gear.

"Don't worry about it," Johnny told me as he retrieved the notebook. "No album is complete without a Duncan Black tantrum. He'll get over it. He knows you're right."

"He said that?"

Con said, "He only ever gets this mad when someone's right about something that he really doesn't want them to be right about."

"That's pretty deep," I said.

"Nah," he said, "that's just Duncan."

I told myself to take their word for it, they knew him better than I did; but I was tense the next night, and it did nothing to relax me when Duncan turned up early and alone.

"Hey," I said. I gave him a brief smile and found something else to look at. "There's coffee if you want it," I said over my shoulder.

He said, "Now who's backing off?"

I turned. "Okay," I said. "It's not my place to tell you what your music should be. I'm sorry."

He pulled a folded piece of paper from his pocket and handed it to me. Watched my face as I read. Saw the song go into me like a lover or a knife.

"So?" he said.

"This is it," I said.

"Yes," he said. "So don't be sorry. Just be…"

I couldn't read his look. "What?" I said: but Con came in, and Duncan shook his head and said, "Nothing."

He gave the song to Con and said, "Read this." Con did, and said *Holy shit*; and later so did Angel and Johnny. They found the music for it that night in a long, intense session. We laid down a rough cut; and when Duncan sang I thought that Lucky was right, it was a problem, and I was ten different kinds of fool.

No one could go straight home, so we ate midnight breakfast at Beth's Café. Duncan sat by the wall, very quiet.

Angel pushed his plate to one side and said, "Anyone want to go downtown?" When he said it like that, *downtown* meant F-tech.

"Laura would kill me," Con said, and turned his wedding ring unconsciously.

Angel said, "It's girl-on-girl night at the Lusty Lady. That shit turns my brain inside out."

"I'll come," Johnny said. Duncan gave him a bedroom smile. Johnny smiled back. "That, too," he said.

"Have fun," Con said. He put money on the table and went yawning out into the night.

Angel looked at us. "You guys go ahead," I said. Duncan shook his head.

After they left, Duncan said, "So why don't you go?"

"Why don't you?"

His brief smile didn't quite reach his eyes. "It would be very second-grade of me to say I asked you first."

I shifted in my seat. Talk of sex had always been play between us, and now I didn't know what to say. *Because F-tech doesn't touch my soul. Because you go home and write a song that does. Because these nights of your music are better sex to me than anything those people do downtown.* True; and too private. But he was waiting.

The only way I could talk about it was by looking at my plate. "Because it isn't real," I said finally. "Well, okay, it is...but it's a game. Put the wire on and someone gets you off. Even if you would never do whatever they're doing, as long as they like it, you'll get there with them. That's fine, whatever works for people...but it's not real to me."

"And what is?" he said.

Having exhausted the possibilities of the plate, I began shredding my napkin.

"What's real?" he said.

I shrugged. There are all kinds of real. It's real to make someone explode out of their own body because you want to, because you can, because it turns you on too. That marvelous feedback is real, whether between strangers or friends. But that wasn't the answer for this night. Not the real answer.

"Your song," I said. His attention sharpened, and I felt the thrill of telling an important truth that sounds inconsequential, of riding the edge of self-revelation. "Letting someone that far in...that's real."

"Ever done it?"

I shook my head. Returned the question with a look.

He shook his head. "Dangerous," he said.

"Like the song says."

"Exactly," he said: and then, "I have to go." He stood and put his money down. Then he leaned into my side of the booth and slid a hand around the back of my neck and put his mouth to my ear and said *Thank you for the song*; and then straightened and said, "See you tomorrow," and left: and I didn't know why I was so certain he was going downtown.

The niece at KCRW, as Jimmy predicted, went gooey over the new album. Nic Harcourt showed it the love on *Morning Becomes Eclectic*, which sent Johnny over the moon. Buzz built. Jimmy set up dates. People bought tickets. The band fought like bears over the set list. The lighting designer got everyone excited simply by knowing his job. We found a rehearsal space and hammered the set into a show. And the week before we left Seattle, Noir played two sold-out nights at Lillie's.

Jenny and I tested the PA and drank sparkling water while we waited for the band to turn up. "Wait'll they see that," I said, pointing outside. We grinned at each other, and when Con's car pulled up we went to the window to watch.

The four of them were in the middle of a conversation as they climbed out of the car, so they didn't immediately see the group of twenty or so waiting at the stage door. Con was the first to notice: the surprise stopped him in mid-sentence, and Duncan, walking behind, had to brace his arms on Con's shoulders to keep from knocking him over. Jenny, standing next to me, snorted in delight. "I wish I had a camera," she said. It would have been a great picture; Con's face was a study in *What the fuck?* followed by *Oh my god*, while Duncan had gone straight to some nascent version of *Holy shit, I'm a rock star.*

The fans enfolded them. Someone handed Johnny a CD to sign. A young man with auburn hair in a ponytail said something to Duncan that made him pause, smile differently, bend close to hear the rest. Angel and Con were cornered by two women in matching leather pants. "Are they *twins?*" I asked Jenny, and we stared, and they were. Jenny laughed so hard she had to sit down.

The house was packed, the energy so palpable that it seemed the air might spark. And the show was terrific; nothing like playing to an enraptured hometown crowd to make a band feel like they own the world.

After the show, Angel landed the twins and sat with them in what, when I passed close, turned out to be an intense discussion of the films of Cordero and Cuarón: *Good for you, girls*, I thought, *make him work for it.* Johnny and Con had their drinks bought for them all night. I lost track of Duncan.

Later, after things thinned out a bit, Lillie and I had a beer together at the bar. The house DJ was spinning slow trance music. There were still a few people on the dance floor, and as I drank I watched a couple sway together at arm's length, talking quietly; then they drifted into the light and it was Duncan and the man from the pre-show crowd. The dancing didn't surprise me; with pick-ups there was always conversation and social touching until the invitation was issued and accepted, but then they would leave. He'd always been private about those things. But now Duncan laughed; and cupped his hands around the man's face, drew him close and kissed him, frankly sexual: eyes half-closed, mouth open, his body looser in the joints. It went through them both like a wave: you could practically see them getting hard.

"Those boys need to get a room," Lillie said, and smiled into her glass; and then saw me watching, and said, "Ah." A pause. "You want some pretzels with that beer?"

"I'm fine," I said. I couldn't help the edge in my voice; nor the clench of regret the next night when the man was back. His hair was loose this time, and there was no dancing: they left right after the show.

One reason for making sure we had good warm-ups in Seattle was that Jimmy decided to open the tour in LA at the House of Blues.

"That's a thousand people," Johnny said on the conference call when Jimmy presented the schedule.

"Don't worry about it," Jimmy said, with a laugh. "That fucker will be packed so tight the girls will have to pee standing up." He cackled, making the phone speaker fuzz with static.

"If you say so," Johnny said.

"I do," said Jimmy. "I know my business. I'm only putting you in places you can fill."

Johnny looked at me. I nodded.

Their nerves were showing before we were even off the interstate. By the time the bus parked in the lot at the Hyatt, across the street from the House of Blues, the four of them could do no more than sit silent and round-eyed like owls until Curtis, Lucky's tour assistant, chivvied them into the hotel.

"Aren't they coming over?" Jenny asked as we crossed the street to the HOB parking lot.

"God, no," the lighting designer, Lucky, and I all said in varying tones of horror. The LD said, "Always keep the artists as far away as possible from anything they can screw up or get ideas about. If it was up to me, I'd scoop them up from the hotel at 7:55 and just throw them onstage." He shrugged.

"Okay," Lucky said as we approached the load-in door, "let's see what kind of trouble we got today."

But there was no trouble: the HOB crew knew their jobs, and one of their lighting guys was already a stone Noir fan. It's always work, but this was smooth work, made fun by the banter of expert strangers who find a rhythm together.

Jenny goggled at the Heritage 2000 mixing console and came close to freaking when she met its friend, the XL250 monitor console. "I can't run that," she said. "It's...big."

"It's the big time, little sister," I said. "We'll go over it this afternoon, you'll be fine."

She wasn't the only one who was nervous: when the band showed up for sound check, sheepdogged by Curtis to keep them from wandering into corners and poking things they shouldn't, Con's first response to the room was, "It's...big."

"It's genetic," I said; and at his confused look added, "Never mind. You'll be fine."

Duncan was in next. He said, "It's *huge* in here."

"You'll be fine," I said.

"I feel sick," he said. But when Noir came on stage and the packed room exploded into noise, he took the crowd with his first clear-eyed *let me make you feel good* look, as if he'd had a thousand people scream for him a thousand times before. The band launched straight into "One Night Soon," and when at least a hundred people began to sing along with the sudden, passionate turn in the chorus, I felt Duncan's surprised laugh bubbling up; I caught it and made sure the audience heard his pleasure and delight. It was a love fest from then on. Angel and Con were mind-melded, Johnny was ecstatic, and Duncan was everyone's lover, everyone's confessor, everyone's voice. The audience danced, sang, and screamed for more; and I felt the music inside Duncan flex and stretch itself to meet them. I heard him at moments sing beyond himself. I saw it make him feel good. And for the first time I thought with utter certainty, *And so it begins.*

We didn't have to leave for San Diego until the following morning, so Jimmy arranged a kickoff party at a West Hollywood club he owned part interest in. I was pleased that many of the HOB crew turned up, and Jimmy filled the place with a nice blend of sincere music fans and gorgeous people with a clear interest in casual sex. And a couple of celebrities as well, to make us all feel shiny.

We had a table right next to the dance floor. People buzzed around us, *Fantastic show, Love the album, Oh my god that song makes me so hot.* Nice for the band: but right now was for us, so everyone was politely turned away while we drank and laughed and dissected the show.

I sat next to Con. Duncan was on his other side, still cranked on music: his eyes shone and his body wanted to touch. I watched the crowd watching us, and said to Con, "So, is this how you imagined it when you were a kid?"

Con made the *huh* face, and then grinned. "The first band fantasy I ever had was that Tico Torres would get run over by the tour bus and I would be Bon Jovi's new drummer."

So unexpected, and so perfect: Duncan and I nearly fell out of our chairs laughing. Con went on, "Seriously. I loved those guys, I still do. And I could totally see myself in the really tight faded jeans and the hair—"

"Stop," said Duncan, who was by now gasping for breath. A wonderful thing, to see him so abandoned to joy. He came out of his chair and straddled Con's lap. "Please, mister rock star," he said, "can I be your groupie tonight?"

"Get off," Con laughed.

"Love to," Duncan said, looking particularly wicked as he always did when he saw a chance to tweak Con, who was undoubtedly the straightest man on the planet.

"You're a fucking pervert," Con said with genuine love. "Get off me." Duncan laughed and went back to his own chair.

"And what did you see yourself playing?" I said.

"Easy," Con said, "'Bad Medicine.'"

"Oh, *god*," I said, so surprised that I told the whole truth when they looked inquiringly at me. "I had sex for the first time because of that song."

"And now you have to tell us all about it," Duncan said.

There was no plate to look at, so I drained my drink instead. "Well," I said, "I could never see myself in one of those high school couple things, you know? My best friends Gabriel and Tara...I was dying for them, but if I'd hooked up with either one that would have been it—Mars is straight, Mars is gay, there's Mars in a box. I wanted it all."

Duncan smiled.

"And I didn't have any idea what they wanted. We didn't know how to talk about it. So we just hung out a lot. Then there was a spring dance, and we decided we wouldn't get dates, we'd go together, no big deal."

"Ah," Duncan said. I could see him imagining me at sixteen.

"We danced all night. I thought it couldn't get any better. And then 'Bad Medicine' came on…"

And Tara gave a rebel yell, and Gabriel said *This song kicks ass*, and we were all three sweaty and loose and out of our minds on music; and although I'd had plenty of sex with myself and a thousand fantasies about them, it was the first time I was ever completely possessed by desire, so that I didn't care who saw or who knew. When we danced, I could see it was the same for them. The song let us say things with our bodies we couldn't say any other way, and we said them all.

"…and an hour later we were all three naked in Tara's basement," I said. My body flared with the memory.

"Mmm," Duncan said. He was watching me as if he could see it like a movie, me discovering myself on a dog-chewed rag rug with a beautiful girl and a beautiful boy.

"Your high school was a lot more interesting than mine," Con said.

And I was suddenly sixteen again, reckless, standing on the edge of myself and burning to jump; so I took twenty dollars and my best smile up to the DJ.

I came back to the table. I took Lucky's hand and said, "Come on."

She looked at me and said, "Are you *dancing*?"

I smiled.

"Oh, yes," she said. Duncan looked a question at me, and it seemed to be a night for unplanned truths: I said, "I do music...and sometimes it does me."

The song began. Con dragged Jenny out to the dance floor, and then entered so fully into the moment that all he could do was jump up and down in place with an enormous grin while she laughed and clapped her hands. Angel gathered up a pair of women from the crowd and put himself in the middle. Johnny and Duncan stayed at the table: Johnny was cuddled up with the HOB lighting guy, a woman with luscious eyes and tattoos everywhere; and Duncan was watching, watching as I opened myself to the music.

Oh, baby, you go, Lucky said, and I turned it loose.

Danced. Surrendered my body to the music as completely as I would to a trusted lover, as I had at sixteen when music and sex and life were so raw, so exciting that I thought I would die of my own jackhammer heart. Tonight, as then, the music was lust and exuberance and joy in being alive, and it danced me down into the hot bright places of myself.

And then a hand on my shoulder; and I turned to find Duncan so close I could feel his heat through my own. It didn't matter that it was a bad idea: music opened my door and Duncan stepped inside, and we began to move with each other, for each other, close, close, never quite touching. We said things with our bodies we had never said before. We danced.

Then the song was done. The others leaned against each other laughing. Con said, "Now that's what I'm talking about!" And Duncan slid his hands around the back of my neck and tangled his fingers tight in my hair, brought his face close: in his eyes, clear hunger for me, and I was fiercely glad even as I thought *What have I done?* His body saying, *I want to make you move that way,* his hands hard on my head, his mouth nearly touching mine, as the endgame trembled between us.

He closed his eyes and took a rough breath. Another. Then looked at me and said in a low, harsh voice, "I can't lose my sound guy."

My turn to drag in a ragged breath; to feel desire twist in me like a brokeback snake. And in Duncan's eyes a flash of anger and pain so brief I wasn't sure I'd really seen it, as his face set, as he very deliberately took his hands off me and turned and walked away.

"Hey," Angel called after him, "where you going?"

Duncan said, in a flat voice, "To find someone to fuck."

Heat came up into my neck and face. I took a breath, folded my arms. Lucky's expression smoothed into marble. Johnny stopped kissing the lighting guy, shot a questioning look in Duncan's direction, and transferred it to me.

Across the room, a table of fans fluttered as Duncan approached. He knelt by a woman and spoke briefly into her ear, then gave her his most disarming smile. She grinned and shrugged in a way I understood very well.

I turned my back on all of it and headed for the bar.

Lucky caught up to me. "What was that?" she said.

"What?" I said, as flat as Duncan.

"No bullshit on my tour, Mars, not even from you," she said. "What was that?"

"That was me getting turned down in front of half of Los Angeles, so you can relax about the fucking tour."

She sighed. "Well, as your tour manager, I'm relieved. As your friend..." She put a hand on my arm. "I'm so sorry."

I nodded and went on alone to the bar, where the first thing I did was bump into someone and spill her drink.

I took a breath. "I'm sorry. Let me get you another."

"No damage done," she said, and laugh lines crinkled around her eyes. "Glenmorangie."

"Nice," I said. I made it clear I wasn't only talking about the brand. When I brought our drinks back, she said, "Will you let me buy the next round?"

"That depends," I said. "Are you affiliated with the music industry in any way?"

"Not at all," she said. "Am I about to be disappointed?"

"Not at all is exactly the right answer," I said. We talked and drank. I forgot her name immediately, but she had a nice laugh. I was glad to find later that she tasted like ten-year-old Scotch all over. I did my best to get drunk on her.

Johnny got me aside the next morning and said, "Are you okay?"

"Sure," I said, in the way that means *Why wouldn't I be?* He let it go, but he was watching. Everyone was. I knew the rules: I sucked it up, did my work, and stayed cheerful.

Duncan and I couldn't avoid each other on a thirty-five foot bus. We were polite and superficial and careful not to touch for several days. Finally, on the road to Houston, I argued with the band about the live mix of "Kill Me Now" and Duncan said, "Okay, you're the sound guy, we'll do it your way," and ran his hand down my arm. He gave me time to see it coming, and I was ready: I smiled just like the old days. Everyone started to relax. And if I became thinner, if I padded up to the front of the bus most nights for quiet 2 a.m. conversations with Carlton the driver because I couldn't sleep, that was my business. Everyone pretended not to notice, the same way they didn't acknowledge that Duncan now sang the angry songs with more bite.

Touring became its own surreal rhythm. We moved from one place to another in a giant bubble of bus and music and the ecstasy of strangers—in the concerts as the band took them with song, in hotel rooms or the lounge at the back of the bus as Johnny or Duncan or Angel took them another way. Sometimes the bus reeked of sweat and sex. Sometimes it seemed to float down the road on a foam of music, whether from the entertainment system in the front lounge or from the band themselves: they liked to play, in all senses of the word, so we'd get everything from Little Richard to the Cure to wicked parodies of Heroes in roughly fifty-mile chunks. Sometimes the bus was a movable feast of conversation fueled by wine and won-der at the sudden turn the world had taken. Sometimes it was a pressure cooker, irritation between people build-ing like steam. It made us harder, more wild, less fit for the regular world. Long days, arguments like squalls that rose suddenly and blew out fast, the fatigue that made people drop expensive equipment, the used needle in the bathroom one afternoon that sent Lucky ballistic; the bad food, the good food, the absolute bliss of a hot shower; the load-outs that seemed unending, the numbing fatigue of one more mile on the bus, the disorientation of waking up someplace different yet again: these things became the stuff of everyday.

But the night. The music. The house heaves with people; the air is thick with their anticipation, their alcohol and musk, the human static of their colliding conversations. When the guitar tech tunes, when I set the mics, the people watch us with a frankness they would never show on the street, as if they could climb into our lives if they only stare hard enough. We're the foreplay; we walk the stage like runway models, racehorses, expert and arrogant and intent, and we stroke your anticipation with every move we make. And when you are ready, when you're panting for it, the band comes to you with hands of music and touches you with heat and hope and joy, with all they know of being human, and it's so big you can't contain it all: you sing and dance and scream it back to them. And then they give you more. Back and forth, back and forth. Ecstasy.

Touching the music was like flying: then came the hard landing of getting back on the bus. The music that scoured and seduced me came on board with Duncan; spun in his eyes, made him smell better, made him move like sex. Made him more elemental every night, so that it took him more effort to ground himself—with food, alcohol, touching everyone in sight, long conversations, dancing, sex—until finally his restless body would quiet and his eyes would be all his again.

Sex was never a problem; fans would have taken numbers and lined up naked in the snow if they thought it would get him naked too, or even just unzipped. But for the rest, he wanted people he trusted to bring him back safely to himself. It was just too fucking ironic that I turned out to be the one who did it best. Johnny and Angel and Con had their own unwinding to do. Lucky wasn't that sympathetic. Jenny was too young to read the cues right; I'm not even sure she understood that the Duncan who came offstage wasn't entirely sane, and I began keeping her with me after shows until I could be fairly sure he was out of the building: when the music was in him, he was a little too ready to explore whatever caught his attention, whatever made him curious.

It started after the Atlanta show. The equipment truck was already on the road; the rest of us waited in the bus for Duncan. The doors were closed against the dozens of fans crowded outside, but we could hear their raised voices; their need crackled in the air, and every so often the bus rocked slightly under their pressure. *Where the fuck is he?* Lucky muttered every five minutes, looking at her watch.

Then the crowd turned almost as one, the way a flock flies, and there was Duncan wandering across the parking lot, his arm slung around a young man who looked moonstruck and walked a little sprung. The crowd enfolded them, begging for a touch, an autograph, a moment of connection: they looked at the young man as if they might chew him into small pieces just to suck the taste of Duncan off his skin.

Duncan pounded on the bus door. Carlton opened it and watched in fascination as Duncan smoothed the young man's hair out of his eyes, said *Bye now* and kissed him. From the crowd, *ohhhh*, and then renewed cries of *Duncan! Duncan!* as he climbed onto the bus. The young man never said a word, just stood wide-eyed as we pulled away and left him with the others in the dark.

"Can I talk to you?" Lucky called. Duncan came over to the small table where Lucky and I sat playing back-gammon and stood behind my chair.

"You're late," Lucky said.

"I promise it was worth it," he said in a playful voice.

"We wait for you because we have to," Lucky said, "and it's fucking rude to take advantage of it."

Silence. Then Duncan slid his hands under the collar of my shirt and began absently to rub my neck. Lucky and I exchanged a look; hers said, *Are you going to make him stop?* But I didn't; I could feel energy passing between us, as if he were hooking a rope into me and pulling himself up from someplace deep. And indeed, after a moment he said to Lucky, in a different tone, "I'm sorry, you're right. I'll do better."

"Thank you," Lucky said.

Duncan became aware of his hands on me, and stilled. I put one hand over his so he wouldn't spook and fall back down the well. He smoothed his palms across my shoulders; stepped back and gave a little shake. Then he was able to sit, drink a bottle of water, kibitz on the game while the last of the music evaporated out of him. Every once in a while he would lean against me to get a better view, or put a hand on mine to help me shake the dice, and each time a small burst like static electricity shocked through me and then disappeared.

Eventually he stood and stretched, and took a deep breath. "Maybe I can actually get some sleep," he said. He looked at me as if turning a question over in his mind; but all he said was, "Thank you, Mars."

"You're welcome," I said, and shook the last small bit of his music out of my hands to show I understood.

After that, he found his way to me more and more often after shows. He seemed to simply need to put his hands on me, and I let him. "Because it helps him," I said to Lucky one day as we sat on a platform in a club in St. Louis, sharing a meatball sub. "And because I'm pathetic."

"I don't get you two at all," she said. "But you're right, it does help. If you can keep it up…because he's…"

I nodded. We both knew he was going deeper down into himself with nearly every show.

Lucky said, "Don't get into trouble."

I bit into my sandwich.

"I mean it, Mars. I'm not even worried about the tour right now. Fuck the tour and fuck Noir and fuck Duncan Black." She licked sauce off her fingers. "Just be careful."

Chicago, Indianapolis, Detroit. People blogged, word spread, and Jimmy began getting inquiries and adding more dates. Memphis, Little Rock. Boston, where Noir opened for Superstition and brought it home to fifteen thousand people.

I don't care much for New York, but the Bowery Ballroom is one of my favorite venues: excellent PA, great sightlines, a perfect room for Noir's brand of intimacy. On the strength of the out-of-town response, Jimmy had already added two more shows the following week, and flown in from the west coast. To oversee the publicity, he said: I figured he had a girlfriend in New York and saw a chance to get tax-deductibly laid.

He took us out for a very nice lunch. Business talk: future bookings, a possible new t-shirt design, media opportunities. Towards the end of the meal, he said to Duncan, "So, Mr. B, hoping you can do me a favor."

"What's up?" was all Duncan said, but he was amused; the corner of his mouth and the slightest narrowing of his eyes gave him away. I'm sure Jimmy had no idea, but it was clear to me. I thought *How do I know him so well?* and hoped someday it might feel like enough.

"Catalina Burnett," Jimmy said, and nodded as if that were the whole conversation.

Duncan made a questioning face.

"Pop music," Con said politely.

"Pop *tart*," Angel said, less so.

"Great girl," Jimmy said. "Just great. Working on a new album now, trying to make her move to something a little more…" He made a *you know* gesture. Everyone nodded. We did. Pop music these days, the audience loves you until you're twenty-two, or they are. It's very sad when people try to hang on longer than that.

Jimmy went on, "Her manager called me today. Catty loves your stuff, she's coming to the show tonight, and she is hoping that you—" an eyebrow to Duncan "—will take her to dinner afterwards. On me, naturally," he added.

"Oh, Jesus, Jimmy," Duncan said. "Do I have to?"

"Is she one of the ones who runs around in no underwear?" Johnny said. "I'll take her to dinner."

"She wants our boy here," Jimmy said. "Her guy thinks hanging out with the summer's hottest indie rock singer will send the message that she's serious about this new direction. And no, you don't have to, but I'd really like this guy to owe me a favor. So maybe…"

Duncan made a strangled noise, but he knew what to say: Jimmy had done a lot for Noir. "Okay," he said.

"Fine." He looked at Lucky. "Will you make a mercy call at midnight and reel me in?"

"You have to be *really* nice to me," she said.

He always loved it when she started a round of the game: I wondered if he knew it was one of the ways she managed him. "That'll be fun," he said, looking devilish. She smiled and waved him off.

"Great," Jimmy said, and actually patted Duncan's arm. "Great. I'll get a car, I'll get a reservation, I'll arrange the tab. You get her there and back and make sure she has a nice time. Thanks, Duncan, really." And off he went, on cell phone to his beleaguered assistant before he was halfway to the restaurant door.

"Oh, god," Duncan said.

"When's the last time you went on an actual date?" I said.

"Oh, *god*," he said.

Jimmy turned up at front of house at ten to eight with people in tow: two big guys in muscle t-shirts, and a medium-tall girl with big dark hair and big dark eyes, short skirt, and not an ounce of spare fat. She looked like a cold would kill her.

"Mars, this is Catalina Burnett," Jimmy said. "Catty, Mars is the best front of house in the business."

"Uh huh," Catalina said in my general direction.

Jimmy said, "Catty doesn't like the VIP room, she wants to watch the show down here." And raised a pleading eyebrow.

"Sure," I said, "come on in." I lowered the security rope so she could step up onto the platform. Her guys gave me hard looks on principle and took up posts on the floor.

"Okay, great," Jimmy said. "Catty, you go on back to the VIP room when the show's over, Duncan will meet you there, okay?"

"Okay," she said. Her attention was fixed on the stage, where Jenny was making final equipment checks. Jimmy left with a grateful look to me.

"Who's she?" Catalina said in the direction of the stage. It took me a moment to work out that she was talking to me.

"That's the monitor guy," I said.

"She's not a *guy*," Catalina said.

"No," I agreed.

"Is she Duncan's girlfriend?" she said.

"Just a second, I'll ask her," I said. I clicked my headset. "Jen?"

On stage, Jenny tilted her head and clicked her belt pack. "Yeah?"

"Catalina Burnett would like to know if you're Duncan's girlfriend."

Jenny burst out laughing, to the interest of the people on the floor.

"I think that's a no," I said to Catalina, and clicked off. Jenny was peering from the stage, trying to get a look at Catalina. Audience heads turned. Catalina stood up straighter; but she wasn't much more than a curiosity to this crowd, although I guessed some of them were speculating about the underwear. I already knew she wasn't wearing any.

Jenny finished her checks and went backstage, still chuckling. Two minutes later, my headset clicked, and Duncan said in my ear, "Tell me she didn't really say that."

"Mmm," I said.

"Shit," he said.

"And tell Johnny he called it," I said.

It took him a few seconds to work it out. "Just kill me now," he said, in such a world-weary tone that I couldn't help laughing.

There was a pause on his end. "I like to make you do that," he said, and clicked off.

Lucky took pity and called him fifteen minutes early, and we were all waiting in the bar when he got back.

"Someone please get me a fucking drink," he said.

"You look a little rumpled there, hoss," Angel said. "Did she take advantage of you?"

"She showed him her underwear," Lucky said.

"She's two years old," Duncan said. "She's about as interesting as a boiled egg. She doesn't even write her own songs. She wants me to help her," and here he did a lethal imitation, "write some totally *dirty* rock and roll, you know?" He shuddered. "Don't even talk to me about her underwear, I was lucky to get out of the limo alive. I'd have to be seriously fucked up to go there." His beer arrived and he drank half of it in one swallow.

"I want to be the singer for a while," Angel said. "I don't have your scruples about emotional intelligence."

"Be my guest," Duncan said. "Cause I gotta tell you, it's getting a little unreal."

Mae West spoke from Duncan's jacket pocket: *Come up and see me.* Duncan fished out his cell phone, checked the caller ID, and answered. "Jimmy, I am never doing that again, okay?" He winced and pulled the phone from his ear. I could hear Jimmy's excited voice from my seat across the table.

"The hotel bar," Duncan said. "Okay." He closed the phone. "Jimmy's coming over."

Jimmy zoomed in about ten minutes later, vibrating with news. "Okay, okay, check this out. I got a guy works for F-tech, let me know a while back they're in development on emotionally-centered tech. Feelings and shit?" He didn't notice the amused look from Johnny, or Lucky's eyes roll: Jimmy was jazzed. "So he brought his VP Marketing to the show tonight." He stopped, hands spread, eyebrows up, as if to say *There!*

"Okay..." Johnny said.

Jimmy raised a suffering look to heaven. "She loved it, she loves you guys, she loves the emotional connection you make with the crowd, e-*mo*-tional, are you with me now? F-tech wants to talk about Noir pilot-testing a concert rig." He ticked off points on the fingers of one hand: "Worldwide media exposure. More audience. Fame. Money. More money." He spread his hands again. "She wants to meet on Monday. I'll send a car at one, be ready, okay?"

Everyone was silent for a moment: Jimmy took that as his cue to stand.

Con said, "Hang on, Jimmy, give me a second to catch up. They want to put people in our heads?"

"They want the crowd to plug into you guys and know what it feels like to be a rock star on stage in front of a bazillion people, which is where you'll be pretty damn quick if you can pull this off. Look, get some sleep, this broad will explain everything Monday, okay? I got someone waiting." And off he zoomed.

Silence at the table until Johnny said, "Wow." Duncan was blank-faced, clearly wandering some corner of his internal landscape. Angel and Con looked at each other, shrugged. "Guess we'll see," Angel said.

The next morning, Johnny made sure that ten copies of the *New York Post* were delivered to Duncan's room, all open to Page Six: *Pop Princess In Private Duet With Rock's Rising Star* under a photo of Duncan and Catalina getting into the limo.

They'd caught Duncan with his mouth open. He looked like a gaffed fish. The band came back from the F-tech meeting looking very much the same.

"So?" I said.

"It's insane," Johnny said, and told me how much F-tech were offering them to pilot the technology. "Small venue, our choice, any date in the next month, full set, plus we accommodate all reasonable media requests. And we get an option to continue repping the tech if everybody thinks it's a good idea."

"Free equipment," Angel said, and I wondered if he was thinking of other uses for it after the shows. Maybe it showed on my face: he shrugged, grinned as if to say *Why not?* It was a measure of the difference success had already made to him that he didn't look at all embarrassed.

"I don't know," Con said. "I don't want strangers in my head."

"It's not like that," Johnny said, as if he'd already said it five times in the last hour.

"What's it like?" I said.

He shifted restlessly. "They say it's like—okay, I come out for the start of the show, I put on the guitar." He made a motion of settling the guitar against his body. "But I'm aware of the audience, they're like this—" and here he turned his palms up, fingers spread wide, and I noticed, as I sometimes did, how sensual his hands were, even more than Duncan's. Sometimes I wondered about Johnny's hands. I felt Duncan's attention: I raised my eyebrow a millimeter and he looked away.

"—this pressure," Johnny was saying, pushing the air toward himself with those hands. "And at the same time I'm checking in with all these guys…it's like I'm focused and wide open at the same time." He spread his hands as if laying the moment on the table. "And when they're plugged in to me, that's what they'll feel."

"Wow," I said. Then to Duncan, "What do you think?"

"I'm curious," he said, and I knew he'd have to have it now, regardless of Con's concerns. "But I don't really know," he went on. "We'll find out tomorrow."

Johnny said, "They want us to do a test run."

Angel said, "We want you to come."

"Okay…" I said, and I'm sure *What for?* was clear in my voice.

"So you can tell us what it's really like," Duncan said.

"Fine," I said. "I'm curious too."

Angel and Johnny brought their own instruments. F-tech had rented a basic backline package with a tech and

202 ∞ Dangerous Space

engineer for everything else. The engineer was territorial, or maybe he thought he was auditioning: either way, there was nothing for me to do but join Jimmy and the company brass and seventy-five or so F-tech employees on the warehouse floor, the largest space in the building.

It took about ten minutes to hook up the band. The rig was wireless so that Johnny and especially Duncan could prowl the stage as usual. They all seemed to settle into it easily, and apart from the glint of mesh through their hair, and the single lead under the left ear, there wasn't much to see.

A man came around with a box of receiver headgear and a smile; he had a lovely mouth, and I smiled back. And again felt Duncan's attention.

"Can I help you with that?" the man said.

"Absolutely," I said, and bent my head so he could fit the gear. He was meticulous. It took a while. His fingers felt good in my hair. Then he handed me the selector that allowed access to each band member, and gave me a thorough demonstration. It was nice to be intrigued by someone's touch.

"Are you a Noir fan?" I said.

"Absolutely," he said, and smiled to let me know he had matched my language on purpose. I've always liked smart.

"Would you like to be my guest at tomorrow's show?" I said.

"You have tickets?" he said.

"I have the best spot in the house," I said, and explained. He said he looked forward to it, and I found I did too; it felt both good and very, very sad, and when I looked again toward Duncan I found him watching me as if he knew that I was beginning to leave him.

"Let's get started," a stick-thin woman said in a voice that bounced in the echo chamber of the concrete warehouse. Every musically conscious person in the room winced, imagining the clatter to come. I felt for the engineer.

The woman nodded to the guy at the F-tech console, and he hit the switch that turned us all on. Duncan gave Johnny, Angel and Con a look that said *Here we go*; and turned to us and said, "Can you feel me now?"

And with the words came a rush of Duncan that may have been all in my brain but seemed to slide down my body, to stream under my skin; and as Johnny played the first chord of "Walk Me Home" I felt Duncan's adrenaline and curiosity and a hum of excited tension; and then, as he reached for the first note, a blast of longing that was the essential story of the song. Many in the audience gasped; and I felt Duncan's deep pleasure in the power to make us feel his music, to make us feel him.

I dialed through them all. Their making the music danced in and out of my hearing it, so that I could feel the musician woven into the song, and it wasn't like being in them at all. They were in me: Johnny's clear joy and the sensual connection between his hands and the guitar; Con's astonishing architectural sense of the beat that made each song something he built around him; Angel's strength of will, and the equal strength of his hands on four strings with which he could open the way to any kind of music. Duncan in me in a way I never dreamed, his music so powerful now that it planted itself in front of my internal door and banged with heavy fists, *Let me in, let me in.*

They played three songs, an emotional range from yearning to anger to a nuanced dissection of love, and when they were done the small audience erupted in big noise and clustered around them, excited, fizzing, wanting nothing more than to maintain the connection. All in the middle of the day in a cavernous room under nasty fluorescent lights. "Fuck me," Jimmy said, "this is gonna be huge."

On the platform, Duncan shook yet another person's hand, turned, and stumbled. Angel caught him. By the time Jimmy and I got there, Duncan was sitting on the edge of the platform with the stick woman peering at him, while Diego of the interesting mouth demonstrated his smarts again by fetching a bottle of water and a damp paper towel.

I knelt by Duncan. "Are you okay?"

He put his hands on my shoulders and touched his forehead to mine, like an exhausted runner leaning on a wall after the end of a race. Only three songs, but the music poured into me: I'd felt how quickly the channel opened in him, how wide. He did a brief internal check and nodded. "I think so. I just got dizzy." He took the towel from Diego and wiped his face.

Stick Woman said, "Diego, please ask Dr. Nuccio to come down."

Duncan said, "I don't need a doctor. I'm fine."

"I have to insist," Stick said. "That's an unusual reaction. We need to make sure you're okay."

"I'm fucking fine," Duncan said; the music talking.

Diego did his best not to smile; Stick didn't blink. "I'm sure you are," she said, "but—"

I touched her shoulder. "Can I speak to you for a moment?"

She didn't like it, but she let me lead her a few steps away. "Send a doctor over tomorrow if you really need to," I said. "If you push it now, you'll lose him."

Stick pursed her mouth. Considered. "Fine," she said: then, to Jimmy, "Call me."

Behind her, Diego mouthed to me *See you tomorrow*.

"That marketing woman is such a bitch," Duncan said back in the hotel bar, a propos of nothing. We all looked at him. He moved restlessly beside me in the booth. His hand had been glued to my arm for twenty minutes; it didn't seem to be helping.

"You liked her fine yesterday," Johnny said.

"Whatever," Duncan said. When it became clear he wasn't going to say more, the conversation turned in another direction. I said quietly, "Are you okay?"

"Fine," he said shortly. "I just..." He moved restlessly again. "Who's the guy at F-tech?"

"Diego," I said. "He's coming to the show tomorrow."

Without warning, Duncan took his hand off my arm and put it under the back of my shirt. He pressed his fingertips into my skin. Bruises tomorrow, I thought, and said, "Take it easy."

The pressure eased: then he leaned close and said, his expression cool and interested, "So you have plans for the delicious Diego?"

"Maybe," I said.

A pause: then he said, "Could you feel me today?"

I'd already told them what it was like. Now I said only, "The technology works."

"Did you like having me inside you?" he said.

A different kind of bruise. I didn't know what to say.

His hand climbed a little higher and dug in again. "Did you like it?"

"Yes," I said. "Now get your fucking hand off me."

"I wanted to feel it too," he said, and ran his finger down my back as he slid his hand from under my shirt.

"Let me out," I said to Johnny on my other side. I think everyone assumed I was on my way to the bathroom; we hadn't even had our food yet. In the safety of my room, I sat on the bed and wondered what the hell was going on. Then I called F-tech and invited Diego to dinner that night.

The Gramercy Tavern has a lovely wine list. Diego rolled the elegant Priorat in his elegant mouth, said *Mmm*, and then asked how Duncan was doing.

"He's actually been a little odd," I said. "Maybe your boss should get that doctor around tomorrow."

He looked concerned. "I hope there's no problem," he said. "Today was a great success. Everyone's excited. I liked their music before, but now it feels..." He couldn't find the words; he put a hand to his heart instead. "I wasn't sure it would work," he went on. "Did you know we had a couple other bands in before Noir?"

I shook my head, drank more wine.

"Very disappointing," he said. "With F-tech, you can tell when people are just going through the motions. One of those bands is really big right now, but they didn't...convince us. But your guys...." He smiled. "Not scared of putting it out there. Very engaged with the music. Very passionate."

"You like passionate?" I asked.

"Very much," he said, and we looked at each other a long moment; then smiled and lifted our glasses again, the evening's course settled between us. Anticipation would be the spice of the next few hours.

Diego said, "I think I should tell you that Duncan Black called me about an hour after you did and asked me to dinner."

"Did he?" I said, as if it were the most common thing in the world, as if my radar were not suddenly on red. "Well, I'm very glad you're having dinner with me."

"I am too," he said, and we moved on to other topics; and then to the rooftop bar at the Delancey; and then to his small apartment, where he was indeed very passionate. A nice person who took his time, who enjoyed himself and me equally: as I rode back to the hotel in the early morning sun, I thought it was real enough. But even as I still smelled Diego on my skin, I also felt Duncan's finger down my spine: *Did you like having me inside you?*

I do better on no sleep than too little, so I showered and changed clothes and went to breakfast. I read the *Post* over my eggs and bacon, and found Duncan's picture again on Page Six, kissing a woman outside a club. *Noir's Duncan Black and friend at Arlene's Grocery. Is the Catalina out of the bag?*

"At least it's a better picture," Johnny said as he took a seat at my table.

"Maybe it'll get her off his back," I said. "The way he is right now, honestly, he shouldn't be let out around the young and deeply stupid."

Johnny nodded. "He's in a place." He studied the menu and said, a little too casually, "Any ideas about why?"

"No," I said.

Johnny looked at me. "Really," I said, "I don't know. Except I think it got a little worse yesterday." But I didn't tell him that Duncan had left marks on my back, or that he had tried to put himself between me and Diego.

The waiter came over with coffee. Johnny ordered a Belgian waffle.

"God," I said, "aren't you a little old to be living on sugar and caffeine?" He smiled and drank his coffee; then put down the cup and said, "Do you think we should cancel the F-tech show?"

"Jimmy would have a fit," I said.

"I'm not asking Jimmy, I'm asking you. Do you think he can handle it?"

I drank my own coffee. I finally said, "I don't know."

I'd invited Diego to show up early if he was interested in how things worked behind the scenes. I gave him the full tour. The house was filling up already—the first show had received orgasmic reviews—and when we walked the stage, Diego stopped in front of Duncan's mic and looked out at the crowd for a long moment. "It must be a hell of a feeling," he said.

We ran into Johnny and Duncan talking in the hall outside the green room. "You guys remember Diego from F-tech," I said.

"Heya," Johnny said, and Duncan gave Diego a *target acquired* smile and said, "I hope you had a good night?"

"Thank you, we did," Diego said, and touched my arm. It was fun to see him score the point, but I wished he hadn't done it, especially when Duncan looked at me in a way I'd never seen before: as if I were a problem to be solved.

It was a strange show; Duncan brought a storm of music to the stage and battered the audience with it again and again. The songs were edgy, violent, wickedly exciting. The music rode him like a loa and he gave himself up to it completely. The audience was frantic with wanting him, wanting the music, wanting more. I wasn't sure for a while that they would let it end.

Lucky stopped by the console after the show. I had just introduced her to Diego when Jenny came from backstage. When I saw Jenny's face, I said to Diego, "Will you please excuse us for a few minutes?"

"I'll be in the bar," he said. He gave Jenny a concerned look as he left.

"What is it?" Lucky said gently.

Jenny looked at the floor for a time. Then she wiped her eyes, took a deep breath and said, "I went to pack up the earpieces like I always do, and Duncan was there..."

"Go on," Lucky said after a moment, her voice a little less gentle.

"I've always had this huge crush on him," Jenny said.

Lucky's face was like a statue. I said, "Tell us what happened."

Jenny crossed her arms and hugged herself. "We were in that little alcove with the gear, and he was being so nice, saying Mars raves about you, and...he kissed me." She regained enough poise to look at us with a wry face. "He's *really* good at it. I just dissolved. And the next thing I knew, I was up on one of the cases and..." Her face was red. "It wasn't exactly private. At least one person came in…I said let's go somewhere else and he said too late, and did I want him to stop? But I…I didn't." She bit her lip.

Lucky and I exchanged a look. I said, "And then?"

"I don't know, he just…he said tell Mars it's my fault you got held up. And kissed me again and said he'd see me later."

Lucky put her hand on Jenny's shoulder. "Did he make you do anything?"

Jenny surprised us both by saying, "He made me come so hard I nearly screamed. No, he didn't, whatever, force me. I wanted to. I just feel so *stupid*." She shook her head. "Right in front of everyone like that. I can't even hardly look at people. And how am I going to be on the bus with him? Jesus."

Lucky produced a tissue from one of her pockets. I said, "Will you be okay?"

Jenny nodded. "This is life on the road, I get that. It's just…it was *Duncan*." She might have been six years old, saying *Christmas*.

"Duncan's an *asshole*," Lucky said.

Duncan opened his hotel room door and smiled when he saw me. Not the nicest smile. Music churned in his eyes, and the strange, edgy energy he'd had on stage curled off him like smoke, but I had built up too much steam of my own to care: I pushed past him into the small hallway of his room and wheeled on him as he closed the door.

"What is your fucking problem?" I said.

He relaxed against the wall next to me and waited, looking interested.

I said, as evenly as I could manage, "I do not have time in the middle of a tour to train someone new. I'm going to have to nurse her through however long it takes her to get over it, and hope to Christ she does."

He said, "Oh, come on, she loved it. She couldn't get her panties off fast enough." He smiled as if replaying a particularly vivid memory.

I said, "She's Con's *sister*, you son of a bitch. She's been crazy about you since she was fifteen, and as soon as her head stops spinning she's going to realize you treated her like a washcloth. You think she's going to love it then? Get real."

He laughed, a brief sound with no warmth; and I said, "I don't even know you anymore."

He looked at me in silence with eyes of wild music; then said, "We can't have that. We need to get to know each other again."

It sounded so reasonable for a moment, until he said, "I know. Let's dance." He said *dance* in a deliberate, freighted way that put us right back in that night in LA; and when he saw that I understood, he put his hands on my head to hold me in place and closed the distance between us slowly, slowly. Gave me time to see it coming. Endgame. Time to hear again Jenny say *He's really good at it* and imagine what I was about to feel; to realize that even after everything, I didn't want to leave; to find myself flooded with wanting as he pressed his body against me, slowly, as he slowly put his mouth on mine.

We never closed our eyes. All through the hungry searching kiss I stared into the music, and it stared into me. When Duncan put his hands on my body, when I put my hands on his, I felt the music roiling through his skin into mine. Slow music. Seismic. Lost myself in it as his hands wandered *adagio* here and there; until one hand slipped into my jeans, and he smiled slowly as the hand found what it wanted, as I drew sharp breath.

He whispered, "Say please."

I stared at him. He bit my jaw lightly and whispered, "Say it."

I shook my head *no*.

"Oh, right, you don't beg," he said, and moved his hand slowly in just the right way, and I made a sound. He laughed. I found enough voice to whisper, "Fuck you."

He smiled a lazy smile, a nothing-but-time smile. "That's the plan," he said, "as soon as you say please. Don't you want to play?" He moved his hand again. "It feels like you do."

Some small part of me that wasn't swamped in sensation was screaming *Pay attention!* My talent, to hear the heart of the matter.

Oh, I thought, *oh.*

Duncan kept his hand stroking slowly, and put his teeth to my neck, and began marking me. It was so erotic that the room went dim for me for a long moment; and then I took a ragged breath and pulled his head away from my neck, held him where I could see him. Thought, *Mars, if you have any courage, find it now.* And said, "Duncan, this isn't a game to me. This is *real.*" I put my mouth on his and said it again, *real*: and kissed him with the word, kissed him slow, kissed him and his beautiful cruel music, and it was like kissing my self in someone else's body. Everything stood still. No breath, no heartbeat, only the *real* of me against him.

His breath caught. His heart pounded against my chest. He stared deep into me. And began to move his hand differently, playing me now like music, lingering, learning me as I shook against him; and I said, *God, Duncan,* and threw the door inside myself wide open. I let him see that in my most private places he would always find himself. I gave him my pride and my talent and my daily joys. I gave him his touch on me that was music, and my touch on his music that was sex. I gave him all my vast longing. All the things that make me Mars. And in his eyes the music receded, and instead there was something like discovery, like recognition: I felt him shake with it, he said *Mars,* and then his mouth fierce on my mouth, my hands on his hips pulling him close, and someone knocked on the door.

It made us both start, and then sag against each other, gasping. I willed whoever it was to drop dead.

They knocked again, harder.

Duncan turned his head toward the door and said aloud, in the roughest voice I'd ever heard him use, "Go the fuck away."

Silence from outside. Then, "Duncan? It's Catalina." A murmur of voices, and she went on, "I've got my songs. And a present."

Duncan looked at me; and with no warning, the connection between us snapped like a bone under too much stress, and his eyes were once again full of mad music. He said, "Aren't you just dying to hear her dirty rock and roll songs?" with such light, ironic loathing that I flinched. A breath. Two. Then he called to the door, "Give me a minute." He said it cold. And pulled his hand carelessly out of my jeans and began working open his fly as his other hand went to the back of my head.

For a moment I didn't believe it was happening; and then I thought *No, not like this, after what I just gave you!* and inside me everything slammed closed. I shoved him hard. He fell back against the opposite wall, swore viciously, and began to straighten his clothes as I went for the door.

Catalina and a young man stood in the hallway. The young man held a shopping bag with several bottles of champagne. He was beautiful, nervous, excited. Catalina wore a low-cut top and hard, bright eyes. "I hope you weren't busy," she said to Duncan in what she probably thought was a sexy voice; then whatever she saw in my face made her step out of my way.

I heard Duncan say, his voice utterly smooth now, "Kitty-Catalina, you look good enough to eat."

"That's totally part of the present," Catalina said.

"Mmm," Duncan said. "Who's your friend?"

"This is Tyler," Catalina said. "He's the other part."

And I couldn't help it; I turned. Duncan regarded me as remotely as if he were an image beamed from light-years away. Then he let the beautiful girl and the beautiful boy into his room and closed the door.

I don't remember going back to the club. I don't remember what I said to Diego. I don't remember finishing my work. I ended up in some bar with Johnny, his guitar tech, and one of the riggers. About three hours after I left Duncan, my cell phone rang. I turned it off without looking at the caller ID. Ten seconds later, Johnny's cell phone played Audioslave. He answered. Listened. Then said to the table, "Anybody here seen Mars?"

I shook my head.

"Nope," Johnny said into the phone, and "Sure," and ended the call and looked a question at me. "He sounded strange," he said.

"Did he," I said.

"Everything okay?"

The guitar tech was watching with great interest. The rigger grinned. "This round's on me," I said, and went up to the bar.

It was almost okay as long as I kept drinking; but eventually I had to go to the bathroom, and on my way back some drunk asshole tripped over his own feet and spilled his beer on me, and I called him a drunk asshole. He said *Fuck you* and shoved past me and was clearly surprised when I drove my elbow into his gut. He dropped the rest of his beer with a wheeze. Some things happened: then Johnny took me to Emergency and sat with me in the treatment room while the doctor F-teched me and found the problem with my ribs. He taped them. He stitched up my split eyebrow and temple and the gash over my collarbone, and F-teched me again. "I think that's all," he said. "But alcohol masks certain kinds of pain." Then he argued with me about making an appointment to get the stitches out.

"I don't even know what state I'll be in," I said. "I'll just take them out myself. It won't be the first time."

"You could make it worse," he said, and shook his head in disapproval when I laughed bitterly. Johnny looked sad and worried.

We traveled in silence back toward the hotel. The taxi spun its way through the wet streets and raindrops ran like tears down the windows. "We have to talk about it," Johnny finally said. "I have to ask. You and Duncan…."

"Were interrupted," I finally said.

He said, "Jesus, Mars—"

"It was him," I said.

His frustration changed to wariness. "What do you mean?"

"I mean I didn't start it. One minute we were arguing, and the next minute he had me up against the wall, and he was very serious. Very." I waved my hand to show I wasn't going there now.

Silence.

"Shit," Johnny said. "Then what happened?"

"Catalina Burnett turned up with a rent boy and a gallon of champagne. And Duncan…did something that made me not want to be there anymore."

"He fucked Catalina Burnett?" Johnny said, as if I'd said something impossible. "What's going on?"

"There's more." I took a breath. "He got to Jenny."

Johnny gave me a disbelieving look. I nodded. "After the show. He was waiting for her. I think he knew it would get me to his room."

"*Shit*," he said, and was quiet for another three blocks. He finally said, "I've played music with him nearly half our lives. I've never seen him like this." He rubbed his eyes as if it would make things more clear. "Why would he…he's worked so hard to keep you."

I didn't know what he meant. I didn't really care.

"You don't get it, do you?" he said. "He never turns down people he likes. Never. We lost our first bassist because Duncan wouldn't say no. But you he says no to. So why, except he doesn't want you to go away?"

"He's got a hell of a way of showing it," I said, and then the fight went out of me and all I could do was lean against the window and say, "Something's wrong with him. You guys need to do something." I felt again Duncan's hands on me the way I'd so long wanted, I saw the music in his eyes, and that other thing that might have been recognition, that might almost have been joy until I saw it break inside him, I saw it break; and I said, "Johnny, he needs help," and my voice broke, too.

He said, "What about you? Are you okay?"

I didn't answer.

"Jesus," Johnny said, "please be okay. Please don't leave us, Mars."

Leave. Step away from Duncan and the music. Or stay, with the meaning of this night between us.

"Please," Johnny said.

I shook my head *I don't know, I don't know*, and I didn't speak again; not even when Lucky dashed out of the hotel bar as we walked into the lobby and saw my face and said, "Did that son of a bitch do that?" in a voice I wished weren't quite so loud. She reached for me and I brushed by, and when she would have reached again, Johnny caught her in his arms and said, "It was a bar fight, Luck, it's okay, come on, it's okay," and persuaded her away as the elevator doors closed on me. It was his greatest kindness of the night.

❦

I spent the morning in my room and took Jenny with me to the club in the afternoon. We put new connectors on every audio cable in the truck. Jenny gnawed her lip and hovered until I said, "Jen, lighten up, I didn't get this defending your honor. It's not your fault." But I didn't blame her for worrying: I looked like a film student's makeup practicum, what with the stitches and the really spectacular bruise across my right cheek. At one point, a roadie called Cheese Grits stopped by with a look that made it clear they'd all heard the story; but he only handed me a twist of paper and said, "Vicodin." I was tempted: my face was sore and my ribs ached, although I tried not to let it show, especially later when Catalina sauntered towards the VIP room in a loose-hipped way that told me more than I wanted to know about how she'd spent her evening. There was a fresh bruise on her throat. I had one just like it. I was astonished how much it all hurt.

I knew the schedule, and I looked at my watch every five minutes, and I thought I was braced; but it was a shock to feel him walk into the room, to know so well the particular weight on my skin of sharing space with him that I could recognize it with my back turned. At least it gave me a moment to put my face in neutral before I looked around.

He was walking toward me, looking wary. Everyone ignored him completely until he passed, then turned to watch him approach me. I don't know if they expected us to kill each other or fuck right there on the floor. I don't even know what I expected. He was so beautiful that it brought right back into me the feeling of his hands, his mouth, his music moving through us. It gutted me. And I don't know whether it was that, or the damage to my face, that washed his careful expression away and left naked regret in its place, so that my heart slammed and I thought *Is he back, is Duncan back?*

He was twenty feet away when Con and Johnny and Angel appeared from somewhere and stopped him. He tried to push past them; Angel shook his head, and Johnny said something in a low voice.

"I need to talk to Mars," Duncan said.

"Later," Con said, in a voice like flint, and took Duncan by the arm. Beside me, Jenny whispered "Oh, shit." Her cheeks were dull red.

Duncan looked at Con in surprise; then at me. "Mars?" he said.

Behind Duncan, Johnny caught my eye and shook his head. And so I said to Jenny, "Let's get back to work," and turned away as the band walked Duncan off the floor.

"Mind if I sit down?" Con said. We were in the area where food was set up for the crew. Con carried two cups of coffee; he pushed one over to me as he sat.

"Thanks for sticking up for her," he said.

I nodded.

"That son of a bitch," he said, and then Duncan stepped in and we turned toward him automatically, as if he were the sun.

I said, "Jesus, what did you guys do to him?" He looked terrible; face drawn and pale, the beginnings of dark circles under his eyes.

Con gave an unhappy shrug and sipped his coffee, never taking his eyes from Duncan. Most of the room was watching him. Duncan didn't seem to notice: he fixed on Jenny, alone at a table in the corner, determinedly hunched over a book and an uneaten roast beef sandwich. She didn't see him until he had nearly reached her: she put her book down with a start and almost spilled her iced tea, and looked up at him with big eyes.

He went down on both knees next to her chair. Her eyes got bigger.

He kept his hands in his lap while he talked in a low voice, and his gaze never left hers. In a minute, her eyes filled with tears.

Con pushed his chair back.

I said, "Let her handle it." After a moment, he nodded.

Jenny's tears spilled over as Duncan continued to speak. And then she leaned into him and cried in his arms while he stroked her back gently, gently; then he buried his face in her shoulder and just hung on.

After a minute, she pushed back and wiped her eyes and said something that made him bite his lip before he nodded. He kissed her cheek. Then he stood and headed for me.

As he neared the table, I said, "If you go down on your knees to me, I'll break your fucking nose." He stopped and didn't seem to know what to do. I shook my head and said, "Go away, Duncan."

"I need to talk to you," he said. "I need us to be okay."

And I could see it as clearly as if it had already happened: the earnest conversation, the apologies, the careful rebuilding, and it all starting over again, and again, and again. *God*, I thought, *one of us has to stop it*. Somewhere deep inside me, a small voice behind a large door might have been saying *No, no:* but I made myself into ice, and his eyes widened even before I said, "Duncan, I don't give a fuck what you need anymore."

Then I got up and left the room.

❧

Jenny found me an hour later sitting in the dark in the back of the equipment truck. I blinked when she opened the door and let the light in. Her face was grave.

"I'm sorry… But Lucky's trying to find you, can you maybe turn your radio on and talk to her? She needs to do pre-show checks. And Duncan's crying in the green room," she said, and then took a closer look at me. "Are you crying too?" she said, with a concern that touched me. Sweet kid.

"No," I said, and wiped my eyes. "I'll call Lucky in a minute. We need to talk, Jen. I've got some specs for you to go over on the bus, and you and I will put in some serious time on the Midas in Hartford. I'll make Jimmy rent you one for the rest of the tour and provide a tech for it. I'll give you all the presets on a card. All you have to do is plug it in and run it."

"Oh, no," she said. "No, Mars."

"You can do it." I gave her the best smile I could manage. "You're a real engineer. Handling things on the fly is part of the job."

"You can't just *leave*," she said.

"I have to," I said.

"No, you fucking don't!" she said. "What did you teach me about the first fucking rule of the road?" Her voice trembled. "You just suck it up, Mars," she said. "You come inside and do the pre-checks and mix the fucking show and then get on the bus and finish the tour."

"I can't do it," I said.

"You *have* to," she said. She was near tears. "Everyone's in there holding their breath. We're all counting on you. Because if you go…it all falls apart. Everyone knows that. Why do you think Duncan's crying?"

"I *can't* do it," I said, and my voice shook, and for the first time Jenny looked truly frightened. I opened my mouth to say *I'm sorry* or *Fuck off* or anything else that would make her go away: and, just as clear as if he were standing next to me, I heard Duncan say in my memory, *I knew I couldn't write these songs. I knew it. And then I wrote them anyway.*

I put my head in my hands for a while. Then I climbed out of the truck. Jenny backed off, pale and silent.

I turned on my radio. "Lucky, come in."

"Heya, Mars," she said. "Can I get some pre-show checks from you?" Her voice was completely controlled, as if she hadn't been at all concerned.

"Yes, you can," I said. "I need about ten minutes, I'll get back to you."

"Thank you," she said. "Curtis? Give the artists the hour call, please."

"Roger, Luck," I heard Curtis say as I turned down the volume. Jenny was waiting by the loading door. I looked up into the evening sky; I heard the buzz of the audience inside, laughter in the parking lot, car horns, someone's radio; the air smelled like gasoline fumes and garbage from the nearby dumpster, and I longed for something clean. I tried to imagine a life where I would ever be happy again. Then I went inside and did the show.

And there we were again on the bus, in quarters too close for me to maintain the space I needed between us. So I talked politely when I had to: my distance was internal, as if I rested in a safe warm place deep inside while some other uncaring Mars lived life on my behalf. I was glass: everyone slid off me. I watched with remote concern as Duncan struggled more and more with the music that was eating him from the inside out: I understood now that his channel was wide open, and sometimes demons found their way through. I watched Johnny and Angel and Con close ranks around him and do their best to keep him safe and sane. All I could do was be true to the music at every show.

It was a blessing that there were only a half-dozen shows after New York: it was time to get back to Seattle and get ready for the F-tech gig. They'd chosen to go through with it because they had a contract, but even more because Duncan became nearly violent at the idea of canceling. And they'd decided to go home, to Lillie's: I thought that was the only good part of a generally bad idea.

"But you'll do it," Con said.

"Sure," I said, and didn't tell them it would be the last one.

Johnny caught me one night as we were walking to the bus. I stopped and folded my arms.

He took a breath. "Thank you…for not leaving," he said. "It means a lot to us that you were willing to keep the band together."

"What are you talking about?" I said.

"Didn't anyone tell you?" When I raised an eyebrow, he got a very odd look on his face. "In New York...we told him if you left, none of us would ever work with him again."

"*What?*" I said. I was surprised to find myself furious: it had been a while since I'd felt anything at all. "What the fuck is wrong with you? You don't break up a band because your sound guy moves on. Jesus."

"You're part of us now," he said, and I shook my head *No.* "You *are*," he said: he didn't understand that I meant *No, don't, I can't take this now.*

"Then why did you stay?" he said. He searched my face. "Oh," he said finally.

I said from behind my glass, "It doesn't matter," and turned and walked toward the bus.

Behind me, Johnny said, as if I'd hurt him, "Mars, it always matters."

"Just one broken heart this time out," I told Lillie. She guessed the rest. "Oh, baby," she said, and gave me a hug and a hamburger with fries.

She had to hire emergency security the day of the gig: fans had camped out overnight in the parking lot, and media people wanted to come inside and get in everyone's way while we were setting up. Things were strained until the F-tech people brought in a portable toilet and set up a free coffee stand, which went a fair way towards reducing tensions.

Diego hadn't made the trip. I wasn't even disappointed. It was best for him: I was leaving Duncan, but I was no longer interested in going toward someone new. Maybe I'd talk my way into the next Heroes tour. Something safe.

And then it was time. Stick Woman came onstage to thank the crowd for being part of "this historic event. Now let's go over the gear..." I tuned her out.

Beside me, Jenny adjusted the wire net on her head. "Are you going to?" she said, indicating the small pile on the console table beside me.

I shrugged. And then I thought, *Suck it up, Mars*. If it was the last time I would touch the music, I wanted it all.

The house lights came down. Lillie's low voice came over the PA. "Welcome to Lillie's, boys and girls. Tonight is a very special night for all of us. I hope you're ready to feel the music of Noir."

I touched them as they took the stage. Con, settling into the drums with absolute confidence. Angel, standing strong, part cocky and part wide-eyed kid. Johnny, even more sinuous than usual, touching his guitar like a lover with those marvelous hands. And Duncan, already full to the brim with music; and I thought that no one in the crowd would sense, as I did, the preternatural strength of will he was exercising to keep it from blowing him apart. I loved him so much at that moment; for fighting as hard as he could, and for everything I knew about him because of the battles he'd already won and lost. *Whatever else*, I thought, *I'll always have this. I'll always know it was real.*

And Con's foot came down, Angel's bass throbbed, Johnny's guitar soared, and Duncan opened himself and began to sing "One Night Soon," and when the audience joined in, I felt how much he loved that they sang his song back to him. The music loved it too: it flung itself into every body and soul in the room. When the song was pain, we cried; when the song was sex, the smell in the room sharpened and people's hands found their way onto each other; when the song was joy, we all flew with Duncan. I loved him for that too, for finding joy even in his most terrible hour.

Noir played. Expert, ecstatic, bound together by love and trust and music. It was legendary to be them on that night.

Nearly done. All of us covered in sweat, all of us feeling the adrenaline buzz that was the only thing keeping the band's exhaustion at bay. We all knew they had given us nearly everything they could. Duncan pushed back his hair and wiped his forehead, and opened his mouth to speak.

And stopped. His expression became totally internal, and I could feel some galvanic struggle within him that I didn't understand. The audience stilled: and where in other situations there might have been snickers or catcalls, here there was only attention and concern; as if we were all willing him to win, whatever that might mean.

Johnny took a step forward; Duncan waved him off. He took a harsh breath and said, with some difficulty, "This next song was hard to write, and I've never sung it the way it deserves. But I will tonight." He stopped again, swallowed, and something in him wrenched, and he said again, "I *will*."

He gave a small wave in Con's direction. The band began the intro.

Duncan looked at me. When his eyes met mine, the jolt of fear that went through him made everyone in the room flinch, and brought me to my feet. All heads turned to follow his gaze; all eyes came to me. I froze.

"You terrify me," Duncan said. Behind him, Johnny's eyes widened; he nodded to Con and Angel, and they kept the introduction going around.

"You just walk right into me whenever you want," Duncan said. His voice shook. "You're so far inside me that you're even in my music. And I've been angry about that, and I have been confused, and I haven't known up from down for a while now; and I've hurt you, and I have hurt myself, and I don't know if you can ever forgive me."

Such grief; then he recovered and said, "I wrote this for you without knowing. You had to point it out to me. That pretty much says it all." He took a breath. "This is 'Dangerous Space.'"

And then he gave me himself with his song. He gave me everything, even as he sang how hard that was for him. He let me see how I made him vulnerable and how that made him angry. How much he wanted me, and how much his music wanted me too. How frightened he was that I would run from his demons and his fears, and leave him with neither love nor music. He opened his private places; and I was there.

And the song ended. There was a moment of absolute silence. And he said, "I love you, Mars."

I felt the truth of it, and his joy that he'd said it; and then I felt something huge and wild rush up in him like a freight train; and he swayed and went down in a boneless heap onto the stage.

I ripped off my headset and scrambled across the console to the stage. People got out of my way. Johnny, Angel, and Con knelt around him saying "Duncan! Dunc—" and I knew Jenny had killed the board. Someone boosted me up, and I went to my knees by him. His eyes were closed. He was pale, still, except for his eyes moving under his eyelids, as if he were dreaming.

"Green room," I said. Angel picked Duncan up as easily as a kitten and carried him backstage.

The green room couch was too short: Angel laid him gently on the rug, and I knelt by him again. Con and Johnny crowded around; Lucky, Jenny, the rest of the crew. I heard Lillie's voice on the P.A. asking people to be calm; a minute later, she was there too.

"Do we need an ambulance?" she said. And everyone looked at me.

"I don't—" I began to say, and Duncan opened his eyes. "It won't let go," he said, urgent, harsh. "Make it let me go." And he sat up with a shudder, put a hand behind my head and pulled me to him hard, kissed me deep and ravenous, shaking, every muscle tight. His music surged through us, so strong, a riptide, and he kissed me as if I were his only lifeline. I broke from him just long enough to say to the others, "Get out," and then his mouth was on mine again and he was tearing at my clothes, my shirt halfway off, his hands on me, and I gave Johnny a desperate wave, *Go, go!* Johnny's jaw set, and he pushed everyone out of the room as Duncan and his hungry music fell on me like a tidal wave.

The struggle to stay afloat in music that only wanted to be out, be free, and didn't care who it drowned. I could feel Duncan trying to hang on, trying not to be lost. He kissed me again and again. He stripped off my shirt and his own, and then I helped and the rest of our clothes were gone and I pulled him to me as the music battered through us. I didn't need F-tech to feel him in me, me in him: the music pulled us back and forth into each other. Duncan clung to me; and it was as if I became the rope he climbed out of himself. I could *feel* him dragging himself up on the part of me inside him, and as he did, the music between us began to spiral, to wail, to pulse: the music on every part of his skin and mine, the music along every nerve in my body and his, and then he was back, Duncan was back and the music wrapped us up, took our breath, made us gasp and shudder and come in each other's arms.

He raised his head and looked at me. Music swelled in his eyes: but he was Duncan again.

"I love you too," I said, and he began to cry.

We lay together for a while, just breathing each other in. Then he raised himself onto one elbow and said, "I finally get you naked, and I don't remember most of it. That's just not right."

"I'll put my clothes back on, you can take it from the top," I said.

"Oh, no," he said. "I'm not taking any chances." He smiled; and then his face changed, he whispered *Mars* and I whispered *Duncan* and we reached for each other. His hands, my hands, everywhere. And when we were shaking from each other's hands, his mouth followed for a long slow while, and he laughed warm and wicked against my skin every time he made pleasure ripple through me, until I pushed him down and showed him how it felt. He laughed then too. And we put our bodies together, we opened all the doors, we found each other inside; and we said *please* so many times I lost count, *please, please,* as the music ran like a river between us.

Noir shows are always packed. F-tech nights are special, but every show is a thrill. When Duncan steps to the

front and smiles to the house, I feel the excitement simmer under my skin. Then he smiles to me. Some in the audience turn to see; the word is out that we are lovers, and
people are curious. They wonder what it's like between us.
They have no idea it begins right here, right now, as surely
as if we were naked in each other's arms. When Duncan
sings. When I put my hands on his music.

Alien Jane

She came in as a thinskin and we started badly. Thinskins pissed me off. Everything about them was hopeless: their screams, their red faces, the smell of their blood; and there was always blood because it was night and they came from Emergency. They made me remember where I still was, and that was a terrible thing, a monster thing with nowhere to go, but boiling out of me in a cloud of rage that fogged me for hours sometimes. The ward is where they put you when you have the rage.

"Don't you bring her in here."

"Calm down, Rita, go back to your own bed."

"*Don't you bring her in here.*"

"Rita, I won't tell you again to behave yourself." Molasses voice and muscles, and she meant it, Madge the Badge, chief white hat of the night shift. The thinskin lay silent as Madge and a no-name nurse made a sling of the sheet under her and moved her onto the empty bed, the one near the door because I liked the window view: it was just the sidewalk to the parking lot, but I could see people walking away. I thought about *away* for a while until the nurses finished with the sheets and the needles and left me alone with her. Then I got up and took the few steps across the linoleum floor.

"You shouldn't be in my room, I don't want you, and if you give me any hassle I'll hurt you, I swear."

She had her eyes closed until then but she opened them wide, bright blue. And she laughed, laughed. She howled. Two nurses came running into the room, and one held her down while the other shot her up, and the whole time she made noise until her face turned purple. They shot me too, I hate that, but the worst was the thinskin and how she scared me.

><

She slept almost the whole next day. I got to where I could shake the sleepydrugs off pretty fast, but she was an amateur, down for the long count. The nurses had her under Close Observation; they came in every fifteen minutes to check on her. "She's still gone, what did you people give her, can I have some?" I kept saying, until they finally made me leave the room. I thought maybe she didn't want to come back up, maybe wouldn't, but later I looked in from the hall and there she was cross-legged in the bed, looking fuzzbrained, the blankets and sheets twisted up around her waist.

"You're up. I've been up for ages. You missed breakfast, you missed lunch but it was crap, lunch I mean, so I guess you're better off, and dinner'll be here soon. You wanna come down to the TV room and watch *Remington Steele*?"

She blinked for a while and then she said, "I have to go to the bathroom." She had a low voice, the kind that always makes me want to practice so I can sound like that. You can talk onto a tape to do it. I used to think about being an actress, but that was all crap too, getting up in front of people and letting them see you cry.

I got my first good look at her while she was trying to get out of bed: older than me, maybe twenty-five, yellow dirty hair, and those blue eyes. She was a mess, bandages everywhere, and where she wasn't all wrapped up she was the pastypale color that white people get when they eat meat all the time and don't work it off. She made my fingers itch to stuff an entire head of broccoli down her throat. She moved slow; and she looked at me. She pulled one leg out of the covers, and looked at me, then the other, and looked, until I finally said, "You see something you don't like?"

She shook her head. "Last night…you said…"

"Oh, *hijumadre*, forget it, I don't like nights and I don't like thinskins, but I won't hurt you. I was just being mean."

"Thinskins?"

"Yeah. New patients, you know, start by crying and yelling that they don't belong up here with all the rest of us really crazy people, which of course they aren't, crazy I mean, and it's all a mistake. Then they get pitiful for a while and won't talk to anyone and shake all the time. They go off if you say boo to them. Thin skinned."

"Right." She was on her feet by this time, more bandage than body. "Well, I'll just have to remember that I belong here," and then she looked like she might cry, which I hate. I started to drift out and let her get herself back, but I don't know, something about her…I don't know. Anyway, I put out one arm and said, "Bathroom's over here," and walked her to the door.

A nurse came in then and took over, she gave me a look and said to the thinskin, "Everything okay here?"

"I didn't do anything," I said.

She was better when I came back, but I didn't want to talk and I guess neither did she, except she said what's your name and I said Rita and she said Jane.

※

She had Dr. Rousseau who was my doctor and the best, not someone I wanted to share with creepy Jane; Rousseau, who half of us would have swallowed rocks for, and even the nurses liked. Rousseau spent a lot of time on Jane, but Jane wouldn't talk much more to her than she would to anybody else, which I respected in a way. She wouldn't even talk to Tommy Gee.

"Does she say much to you when you're together on your own, without any doctors around? Does she seem to communicate better with her peers?" Tommy Gee was always doing that, mixing up the stupid patients talk with the doctor talk so you never knew if he meant it for you or some white coat standing behind you. His real name was Gian-something-Italian but we called him Tommy Gee-for-gee-whiz because that's how he was about everything, including being Rousseau's intern.

"If you mean does she relax when she's with the rest of us mentals then no, Dr. Gee, I guess she isn't comm-you-nee-cating well at all. Maybe they don't talk on whatever planet she's from."

"That doesn't sound very supportive, Rita."

"You're the doctor, you support her."

And he tried to, he was always coming around after her sessions with Rousseau, to talk to her, see if there was anything he could do to get her to open up. She was his special project.

I got used to having her in my room because she was so quiet I didn't notice her half the time. I talked to Rousseau about that in one morning session, and she just said *hmm* and wrote it down.

"I think Tommy Gee likes her, too, but she probably hasn't even noticed how stupid he gets around her."

"Hmm."

"I guess it'll be okay having her there, I mean, I probably won't even notice when she's gone until two days later."

Rousseau put the cap on her pen and sat back in her chair. There was a little mended place near the pocket of her doctor coat. The first time I saw Rousseau was twenty hours after I came into Emergency, when they moved me up to the locked ward. She asked me if I wanted to talk and I said no like always, feeling like a rock in the gutter when the rainwater runs over it pushing it little by little toward that big dark hole going down. I said no, and then I saw the mark on her coat, the careful clumsy darn, and I could never explain how it made me feel; but then it was okay to talk to this woman Rousseau.

She turned the pen over in her fingers, gave me a doctor look. "Haven't you thought you might be the first to leave?" she asked.

❮❯

I spent the rest of the morning like always, huddled up with Terry Louise on the bench down the hall from the nurses' station: her smoking cigarettes until she could hide behind the cloud they made; me trying to get my back comfortable against the wood slats, and making kissy noises at the boy orderlies when they went by, because I hated the way they always picked on the little scared ones to rub up against when they thought no one was looking. They walked itchy around me after what happened that one time.

"I hate it when she does that," I said. "Why does she have to talk about me leaving?"

"Just say no, babe," Terry Louise said through a mouthful of smoke.

"Can't keep saying no forever."

><

Jane's bandages came off, and she was all new pink skin on her arms and legs, like someone had decided she was a big fish that needed scaling. "She did it to herself," Terry Louise said one morning from behind her smoke.

"No way."

"Uh huh. Why do you think she's in here? This isn't a plastic surgery ward."

"No one has the guts to do that to themselves. There's no way she could have got past the first leg."

"Madge the Badge was talking to one of the student nurses last night. So unless the meaning of self-inflicted has changed while I've been away, No Brain Jane is sicker than we are."

"We're not sick."

"Stop squirming around and sit still for half a minute, Rita, you look like something I'd like to bait a hook with," Terry Louise said. The old scars down the inside of her dark arms showed plainly when she raised the cigarette to her mouth. She smiled.

><

Susan came to see me over the weekend. She made me feel like she was holding my soul when she touched me: I wished Jane would disappear, but she was right there, watching.

"Suze, this is my new roommate Jane." I rolled my eyes, but not where Jane could see.

Susan leaned across the gap between our beds and held out her hand. "Hi."

Jane picked lint balls off her blanket.

Susan stood with her hand out. Jane wouldn't look at it.

"You shake her goddamn hand, you pink turd; I'll hurt you worse than whoever did you the last time."

"Rita, shut up." Susan put her hand down. Jane was shaking and squeezing her fingers open and closed around great fistfuls of blanket. Her eyes were shut tight, so she didn't see me reach for her.

"*Back off, Rita.*"

Susan got me out of the room, down the hall. She left bruises on my arm.

"Don't hang onto it. I don't care, I don't even know her. Anyway she must be hurt pretty bad."

"Fuck her. Everybody's hurt."

That was all it took to spoil my day with Susan, just ten seconds of goddamn Jane. When Suze finally left we were both strung tight, dancing around each other like beads on a wire. I glided back into my room like running on electric current.

It came out at Jane then, all my meanness in evil words, and Jane just closed her eyes and bit down on her lip to keep from crying; and when I finally stopped, she opened her mouth and said something that might have been *I'm sorry, I'm sorry*, but it was hard to tell around all the bright red where she had chewed her lip right through.

><

The lip needed stitches. "Frankenjane," Terry Louise chortled up and down the hall, "Franken-jane, feels no pain."

"Shut up, Terry Louise."

"Well, excuse me, honey, I meant to say *Princess* Jane. Princess Jane, so insane—"

"Shut up!"

"Humph," Terry Louise said, and lit another cigarette.

"She didn't even know she'd done it."

"I know, you told me seven times already—"

"She practically bit her lip *off*, I could see her teeth right through it, and her tongue was all dark red—"

"Rita—"

"Rousseau said it wasn't my fault, but we all have to be careful, we have to be careful, she's always getting hurt and not knowing because she can't feel the pain and you were right, she did that other stuff to herself, to her own self, it's sick, how could anyone do that and not feel it, it's sick, she just chewed herself *up*—" and I couldn't stop talking, faster and faster, couldn't stop even when Terry Louise ran for Madge the Badge.

It took a long time to wake up from the needlesleep the next day. I was still in bed when Rousseau and Tommy Gee came in with Jane. I wanted to open my eyes, to say *I'm sorry*, but the drug was like a staircase that I had to climb, and every time I got to the top I would be back at the bottom again: like big wheels in my head turning all night, so I was more tired than if they had just let me cry for a while.

"Thank you for seeing Dr. Novak," Rousseau said to Jane. "Do you have any questions about the kind of testing he wants to do? I know he might not have explained things completely, he's so excited about your condition...."

Jane was quiet.

"Please understand how important this is," Rousseau went on. "No one here has had the opportunity to examine congenital insensitivity to pain; it's very rare, and there are so many things we want to know...."

"I'm not a lab animal."

"No, you're not. No one will treat you that way. You're a person with an unusual condition, and with your help we can learn the best ways to deal with other people who have it. We may be able to help you find ways to live with it. I promise no one will hurt you...I mean..."

"I know what you mean, Doctor." Jane sounded a hundred years old, tired and thin-voiced.

"You don't have to do this if you don't want to. No one will make you," Tommy said gently.

"Will you excuse us for a moment, Jane?" Rousseau said. I felt her and Tommy move past me toward the window, their footsteps sending small shudders through the bed and the bones of my skull.

Rousseau kept her voice low. "Tommy, I expect you to back me up on this."

"I just don't think we should push her. She's only just started to connect with us. It's a little soon to ask her to include someone else in that trust."

"Dr. Novak is one of our best research neurologists. I think we should be supporting Jane's opportunity to work with him."

There was a silence that seemed long.

"I don't understand why you're doing this. I know you don't support his research funding, you even wrote a letter about it to the Chief of Neurology last year."

"How did you know about that?"

"Everybody knows."

Rousseau's voice suddenly sounded very close, sharp. "Great. Then maybe everyone should know that I have since retracted that letter and encouraged several of my patients to participate in Dr. Novak's studies. Including Jane, if she's willing."

"I still don't think—"

"Thank you, Doctor," and that didn't sound like any voice I'd ever heard come out of Rousseau; *What's wrong* I wanted to say, but I couldn't open my eyes. I heard Tommy Gee thump out of the room.

Then Rousseau took a deep breath and walked past me to Jane's bed.

"I just need you to sign this release."

I knew I should open my eyes, but I couldn't stop climbing stairs inside my head. *No*, I tried to say, *no no*, but I could only make a little noise. "Go to sleep, Rita,"

Rousseau said, and pulled the curtain across between me and Jane.

※

She became Silent Jane again, and I saw less and less of her because she had started the testing, and once the lab rats got hold of her they didn't want to give her up. The nurses talked about it up and down the halls, even Madge who was such a porcupine for rules; so we all heard about Jane in the lab being electroshocked and pinpricked and nerve-pressed and never feeling a thing, and how it was something you were born with, and that nothing that happened to you ever hurt, no matter how bad it was. Terry Louise said it was kind of neat, and Jane was like the star of one of those old flying saucer movies where the alien takes over your body, so you look like a human but you're not.

※

One day in the room, I wanted to say I was sorry.
"Forget it."
"I didn't mean to hurt you."
"Stupid. Stupid, stupid. No one can hurt me. They've been trying for a week now. Go ahead, do your best."
That wasn't what I meant, I thought, and I couldn't think of anything to say, so I just went on sitting on the edge of my bed rubbing my fingers down the little nubby rows of the bedspread. Jane lay on her back, arms straight by her sides, toes pointed at the ceiling. Her pajamas were dirty around the seams. She looked very thin, greasy with fatigue. She kept absolutely still. She moved only to breathe, and she wouldn't look at me.

I thought I would lay down too like that and look at the ceiling, and be very, very still. The ceiling was grey and restful. I wondered, if Jane and I lay in the same room long enough, would we start breathing together? When I closed my eyes I could hear everything. I heard orderlies wheeling medicine carts past our open door, the pills hissing in the tiny paper cups, little insects full of honey and poison; nurses in rubber soles; Terry Louise in paper slippers; Tommy Gee in his pointy leather shoes; Dr. Rousseau in heels: all stopping at our door, heads bent around the jamb looking in at Jane and me laid out like bodies on the back tables of funeral parlors, waiting to be made pretty enough to be seen by the living. *Go away*, I thought, *go away*, and they all did, while Jane and I breathed together and the morning turned grey under the weight of wet clouds and the light in the room dimmed into something soft and private.

After a long time the old pictures came back into my head, and this time it was okay to let them move through me with the sound of our breath like slow waves on a beach. The pictures turned into words, and I told myself to Jane.

"When I was little I wanted to wear jeans and climb up the big oak tree onto the garage roof and play pirates for the rest of my life. I could see everything from there. I thought I was queen of the world.

"Down the road from us was a big field where the grass grew as high as my waist, all green and reedy, so it whispered when the wind went over it. I would run through it with my arms flung out wide, as fast as I could, so the wind would pick me up and fly me away. But I would always lose my breath too soon and fall down into the green

244 ∞ Dangerous Space

and the smell of warm wet dirt with just a strip of sky showing overhead, and I would have this whole world that was just for me, just mine."

I breathed gently and thought about my green place, and Jane was there; I could feel her in the grass wanting to run.

"When I was twelve, they took it away. They decided it was time for me to start being a girl like my sisters and my mother, and they made me put on a dress and shoes that hurt my feet. I knew I could never run in those shoes. I said I wouldn't do it; I was standing in the dining room in these clothes that felt like ropes around me, and I said I won't, I won't... My father locked me in the hall closet with the winter coats. It was dark, and I couldn't move in those clothes, and the shoes were too small, they hurt.... I think it was those shoes did something funny to my mind. I think they were why I hung my Christmas doll up by one foot over my father's favorite chair in the living room and set fire to it...to the doll, I mean. I lit the match and put it right up against the hair and the whole thing melted and dripped onto the place in the chair that was rubbed shiny from my father. The house smelled for weeks.

"Then I was always in trouble. Always fighting. I burned more things, I tried to run away. I hurt my little sister bad one time with a rake. Everything just got worse. It's better now I'm not with them anymore."

Jane said nothing.

"Maybe it's better you're here now."

Jane breathed.

"I stole things, I got caught. My parents gave me up to the court. My mother cried, said she couldn't do anything with me. She's Catholic, she'll carry it forever. I spit at the judge. That's what got me away from my folks, spitting at the judge. He didn't care about the broken windows and the badmouthing and the knife that time...he just didn't like me spitting at him. Spoiled his day."

Maybe Jane smiled, maybe not.

"But it all just hurt too much after a while. When you fall down out there in the world it isn't green and soft, it hurts.... I met Suze in that place for girls where they sent me...but it was too late and I felt so bad and I tried—"

I thought of Jane's legs and arms.

"They have to put you in here for that, and at first I hated it, it was like the closet again. But now there's Rousseau and Terry Louise.

"I don't do those things anymore, not really. I still... you know, I still say things sometimes, but even then it's like I only do it to make myself feel bad. I guess the meanness is going out of me. Rousseau says I'm better. She wanted me to leave a few months ago...but I screwed up, I did it again...one of the orderlies, that stupid Jackson pissed me off. But I could have been out only I...I couldn't remember anymore how it felt, running in the grass."

Wax Jane, silent Jane. Ceiling-staring Jane.

"Suze is what I have left. If I mess that up I don't know what would happen. So I get funny sometimes. I guess you don't have to shake her hand if you don't want to."

I closed my eyes. It surprised me when she answered. Her voice sounded like she hadn't used it in a long time.

"I saw how she held you, how she touched you, you know? And I thought...how lucky you were that someone would touch you like that. And then she held out her hand to me...I couldn't take it. It would kill me right now to have anyone be that nice to me. I'd rather spend all day with those doctors poking wires in me than one second with your girlfriend's hand in mine."

There was something in the way she said it; I saw again my father's face when he found the doll in a stinking puddle, and my mother saying *How could you, how could you*, but never answering her own question. Jane reminded me of how the world can be so different sometimes from what we expected. I got up and poured her a cup of water and put it on the table by her bed. I knew she wouldn't want me to touch her, even though I would have liked maybe just to hold her hand, not like with Suze, but only because she was scared and in a lonely place. I crawled back onto my bed and turned on my side away from her, blinking against the light. I thought that in my life I had been little Rita, and Rita full of rage, and crazy Rita, and now maybe I would be some other Rita: but I couldn't see her, I didn't know if she would be someone who could run through the world and not fall down.

❧

Rousseau came into my room the next morning. She looked funny, and she said a strange thing: "Rita, please come with me down to the lab."

"Why?"

"Jane is asking for you. I'd like you to go be with her, if you don't mind."

We walked down the hall. Rousseau started for the elevator and I said, "I want the stairs, okay?"

She turned back so fast she almost caught Weird Bob's visiting sister with her elbow. "Sorry, I forgot about the claustrophobia." She didn't apologize to the sister. That and the forgetting and the asking in the first place made three strange things.

We walked down the stairs. I went first. "Three floors down," she said. She was close, only a step or two behind me. Her smell came down over me like green apples.

"Rita...you know that Jane agreed to work on these experiments with Doctor Novak. She's a volunteer. I just want you to remember when you see her...I don't want you to think...she isn't being *hurt*...." she said in a queer, rushed voice that didn't even sound like Rousseau. I stopped. Her hands were jammed into the pockets of her white coat, and her face was turned to the wall, and she wouldn't look at me.

That was the strangest thing of all, and it scared me. It wasn't Rousseau standing over me, her red hair sparking under the stairwell light. My doctor wasn't scared; my doctor was an amazon, a mother confessor, a carrier of fearlessness that she would breed into me like a new branch grafted onto a young tree. My doctor wasn't this person who was saying, "Just be calm and don't worry, everything will be fine."

"What's the matter with her?"

"Let's go."

My slippers rustled on the stair tread and on the linoleum of the hall when we went through the landing door. I followed the stripes painted on the wall, around and around the hallways like a maze. We came to a locked ward door and a nurses' station beyond it. The two men behind the desk wouldn't let me in until they checked with Novak on the telephone. The brown-haired one had a badge with a metal clip that he tried to put on me, and I wondered if I would have to hurt him, but Rousseau said, "Don't touch her."

"Doctor?"

"Let her put it on herself."

Brown Hair rolled his eyes and handed me the badge dangling between two fingertips, arm outstretched. Rousseau said nothing, but she was shaking just a little as we went down the hall, we could hear Brown Hair say something to the other one, and they both laughed, and I didn't like being there at all, in a place I didn't know, with strangers.

The hall was long and mostly bare, with only a few metal-backed chairs next to closed doors. The air smelled like ammonia and sweat and burned electrical wires. It was quiet except for our breathing, the *rsshhh rsshhh* sounds of our clothes and Rousseau's hard-heeled, strong step. Then I began to hear another sound, a rise and fall of muffled noise like music, but something about it made me want to walk faster, and then it was Jane screaming and I began to run.

The place where they had her was at the end of the hall, a high-ceilinged room that made an echo out of Jane. The lab was full of white: white-coated doctors, orderlies in white pants and shirts, Jane in her cotton pajamas with her rolling eyes that showed white and blue, white and blue. She sat in a wooden chair with a high back and arms. Thin rainbows of color twisted out of her head, wires running out of her scalp into the machines around her. More wires with small discs on the end lay taped like lollipop strings against her neck; her left wrist; her pink-scarred calf; her ankle; under her pajamas at her heart. She sat very straight in the chair because her shins and forearms and ribs and head were belted against the wood with padded ties the color that white people call flesh, and I wondered if they thought that no one would see the ties because they were the flesh of Jane. Jane was screaming around a rubber mouthpiece that showed tan and wet from her saliva every time her lips pulled back—not terror screams but more like some giant grief, some last precious thing taken away. The room was full of her smell.

I couldn't go in. I stood at the door and I couldn't step into what I saw in that room. Everyone except Jane had stopped in mid-motion; they stared at us with the glazed otherplace look of people caught in the middle of some terrible thing like rape or butchery, the kind of act so horrible that while it is happening the doing of it removes you from all human space. I tried to turn around, but Rousseau was right behind me with her hands braced against the door frame, leaning into it like she would push the whole thing down. Then there was nowhere to go but ahead.

"Goddamn it, goddamn it," Rousseau was muttering as she moved in behind me.

"What are they doing, what are they doing to Jane?" I said but she didn't hear me. Novak came over and stood in front of us like he was trying to keep us from coming any further in.

"Jesus Christ, what is happening here? I told you to stop the goddamn test until I could get back." Rousseau's voice was low. I felt squeezed between her and Novak.

"Calm down, nothing happened, she's just upset."

"She's still my patient. You had no right."

"Nobody has done anything to hurt her. Christ, Elaine, I'm a doctor, I don't—" Jane stopped screaming, suddenly, like a light turning off. Spit ran down her chin. The machines buzzed and the paper strips whispered onto the floor. A woman with a needle stepped over the coiled electrical cords toward Jane, and I could feel myself tense.

"It's okay, Rita," Rousseau said. "I'll get someone to take you back to the ward."

"No." I pulled out from between them, went toward Jane. Behind me I heard Rousseau start in on Novak. I felt proud of her again, fighting for Jane; then I was standing in front of the woman with the needle and she turned toward me. "Leave her alone," Rousseau said, and the needle went away. Jane saw me and tried to move. I didn't know if she was trying to get away or get closer, and for a moment I remembered the Jane who didn't want to be touched in love, the Jane who would rather stay different in her wires and straps, apart from people, alien Jane; and the Rita who always reached with hurting hands. Then I unbuckled all the straps and put my arms around her, and she didn't pull away.

The other people in the lab began to move then, but they didn't seem to know what to do or where to go. I didn't want them to touch Jane but they did; they took the wires off her head and peeled them off her legs. They had to reach under me to get to her arms and chest. There was a piece of metal under one white bandage on her arm. They took the metal and left the bandage. They took the mouthpiece, but no one wiped her wet chin so I dried her with the corner of my robe. There was a funny smell about her, something burning; fear-sweat, I thought.

Rousseau came over, with Novak following. They squeezed around me. Jane closed her eyes.

"Let me see her, Rita." And so I had to let go. My hands still felt full of her even when they were empty.

Rousseau said something to Jane I couldn't hear. Jane shook her head, eyes still shut, face pale and moist under the hot lights.

"What's this?" Rousseau said.

She had found the bandage on Jane's arm. When she peeled it back, the arm was white around a stripe of red, and in the center of the stripe was a blister, raw and runny. The smell was worse with the bandage off.

Rousseau looked up at Novak. Being next to her made me feel cold.

"It was an accident," he said. "We were testing her for heat response, one of the techs pushed the dial up a little too high." He shifted, jammed his hands into his coat pockets, rolled his eyes like he thought Rousseau was being ridiculous. She still hadn't spoken. She was so tense I thought she might break apart if she made a sound.

"Oh, come on, Elaine. Nobody got hurt."

"What do you call this?" Her voice was very soft.

"I call it an accident, for chrissakes. It's no big deal. She didn't feel a thing."

Jane began to cry.

Rousseau put the bandage back over the wound and smoothed down the tape. She stood up. "I'm reporting this," she said to him, still speaking softly. "I won't let you harm one of my patients, not that." It was like she was talking to herself.

"She's not really your patient any more."

"You can't do that."

"I already have. She signed the consent form; she's a volunteer. I can do her a lot of good."

"You don't have enough clout for this; I don't care what strings the Chief of Neuro pulls for you this time."

"Try me," Novak said. "But you'd better be ready, Elaine, because you'll have to go across country to find a job after I'm finished with you."

"Jesus," Rousseau said thickly.

"Jane is the professional opportunity of a lifetime," Novak went on, "and you don't have the slightest idea what to do with her. But I do."

It felt like a punch in the stomach, the sick-making breathless kind. *It isn't true*, I wanted to say, and then I saw Rousseau's face like still water, and I turned away so I wouldn't have to watch while Novak put one arm around her and led her away, saying softly, persuasively, "Don't be upset. I didn't mean to upset you. Jane will be fine with me, I promise, she'll be fine, and you can still manage her therapy, keep an eye on her, why don't we just go have a cup of coffee and talk it over," and I moved closer to Jane and she grabbed me, pulled me in, and I realized she was whispering, her voice becoming more clear as Novak and Rousseau moved away.

"...it keeps you safe, keeps you safe, the pain keeps you safe, because it hurts and you know something's wrong. People like me die if we're not careful; we pierce our lungs with a broken rib we didn't know we had; we smile and eat dinner while our appendix bursts inside us; we hold our hands out over the fire when we're children and laugh while the skin turns black. Pain keeps you safe. It's how you keep alive, how you stay whole, it's such a human thing, and I don't have it. I don't have it. And you people...you think...no one ever asked if I could—but I can, I can, I can feel a touch or a kiss, I can feel your arms around me, I can feel my life, and I can feel hopeful, and scared, and I can see my days stretching out in this place while they forget and leave the heat on too long again and again and again, just to see, just to see me not knowing until I smell my own skin burning and realize. And when I look at them they aren't human anymore, they aren't the people who bring me ginger ale and smile at me. They're the people who turn up the dial...and they hate me because I didn't make them stop, and now they have to know this thing about themselves. They'll never let me go."

I held her tight. "Tell them," I said. "Tell them like you told me. You can make them stop, Jane, you don't have to—"

"I do have to, Rita, I do, I have to be... I keep thinking they'll find a way to hurt me like they want, something that will work, and then I'll be okay, I'll be safe, I'll be like everybody else, and I won't have to be alone anymore."

And then I understood that the smell in the room and the rawness under the bandage was her pain, her alien pain; and I suddenly saw how she might have taken a knife and stripped her own skin away, earnestly, fiercely, trying to see what made her different, find it and cut it out, and take away the alien and just be Jane.

I held her. There was nothing I could say.

➤✦

The next day Jane was transferred to the locked ward upstairs. Tommy Gee didn't want to let them take her. "There's a mistake," he said. "Wait for Dr. Rousseau. She'll be here in just a minute." But I knew she wasn't coming. "I'll find her," he said, and went running down the hall.

Jane stood just inside the room, one step from the hallway that would take her further inside her fear and her need, and she smiled. "I'll come see you when I'm better," she said. "You and Susan."

"Yes," I said.

"We'll go to the beach," she said. "We'll spend all day. We'll swim and lie on a blanket and eat sandwiches from a cooler. We'll get ice cream. We'll go for a walk and find crabs and sand dollars. We'll get sunburned and you'll press your finger against my shoulder, it will stand out white and oh, I'll say, oh, it hurts."

"Yes," I said, "it will hurt."

She looked at me like she was flying, and then she went out the door.

I found my jeans and a sweatshirt and sneakers and put them on, and packed my things into my duffel bag that had been stuffed into the back of the closet for so long. I went down to the nurses station, passing Terry Louise on the way. "Where are you going?" she said.

"To the beach."

"What?"

"Bye," I said, and I could feel her watching me all the way down the hall, so surprised she forgot how much she liked to have the last word.

"You can't leave," the day nurse said uncertainly.

"This is the open ward, *amiga*, I can walk out of here anytime I want."

"You aren't a voluntary patient, you have to have your doctor's signature."

I don't have a doctor anymore, I wanted to say, and then Tommy Gee was there looking pale and tense. He saw my bag.

"I'll sign for this patient."

"Did you find Rousseau?" I said.

"I talked to her." He looked past me down the hall. "She's gone."

I wasn't sure who he meant, Rousseau or Jane, but I nodded.

><

I walked down five flights of stairs to the lobby entrance doors, and stopped. I looked back across the open space, full of people with flowers, new babies, people sleeping on couches, people crying, people going home. Two women went past me, one with a new white cast on her arm, the other one saying, "Are you okay? Does it hurt?"

The hurt one bit her lip and shrugged. "It doesn't matter."

"Oh yes it does," I said. I walked to the door and thought, *I will be Rita running in the grass*, and took the first step out.

Biography

Kelley Eskridge is a fiction writer, essayist, and screenwriter. Her short stories have been finalists for the Nebula and Tiptree awards, won the Astraea Writer's Award, been collected in *The Year's Best Fantasy and Horror*, and been adapted for television. Her novel *Solitaire* was a *New York Times* Notable Book, a Border Books Original Voices selection, and a finalist for the Nebula, Endeavour, and Spectrum awards. A movie based on *Solitaire* is currently in development.

She lives in Seattle with her partner, novelist Nicola Griffith.

www.kelleyeskridge.com